STATUS

STATUS

By

Jordan Belcher

Felony Books, P.O. Box 1577, Belton, MO 64012

Felony Books, a division of Olive Group, LLC,

P.O. Box 1577, Belton, MO 64012

Copyright © 2013 by Jordan Belcher

ISBN-13: 978-0-9851903-6-1

Library of Congress Control Number: 2012956574

Felony Books 1st edition February 2013

10 9 8 7 6 5 4 3 2 1

Manufactured in the United States of America

For information regarding special discounts for bulk purchases, please contact Felony Books at www.felonybooks.com.

CHAPTER 1

With the tap of her thumb, Quita Wheeler loaded up one of her favorite websites, a social media page called The Site. She scanned through her news feed until she saw a status update that brought a huge smile to her face.

"Rodrick!" she called out from her bed.

He didn't answer.

"Rodrick! Come here! Look at this!"

He still didn't respond, so she threw the covers back and scurried through her apartment in the nude. She found him in the living room on his knees, facing the window. He wasn't fully dressed either. All he'd thrown on was his 501 Levi denims, and they were a little baggy, exposing the top of his butt crack. The first time she saw him in this position she thought he was sick. But she knew now that he was praying. And she knew not to interrupt him. He had grabbed her by the throat and cursed her out the last time she did that.

"Amen," he finished, standing up.

"Why do you always do that?" Quita asked him.

"Do what? Pray?"

"Yeah. Every time after we have sex, you come in here and pray. Why?"

"Because I've sinned."

Quita followed him as he walked back into the bedroom and got his clothes on. He was one of the handsomest men she had ever slept with. She didn't just think he was handsome because he had money either. His arms had hints of muscle, but his gut was semi-small and beetled; he was beautifully flawed. From the amount of time he'd spent behind bars, she expected him to be covered in prison tats. But he had not a one. He shook his neatly done dreads after he slipped on his T-shirt. Then he capped his dreads with a Louis Vuitton beanie hat.

"What did I tell you about interrupting my prayer?"

Her eyes shifted nervously. "I thought you were in the bathroom. I didn't know you were praying."

"But you just said you knew that after every time we have sex, I pray. Why would this time be any different?"

"I ... my mind wasn't—" she stammered. "I'm sorry, Rodrick."

"So what was so important?"

"This." She handed him her phone. "I thought you were playing when you said you loved me. But this confirms it. You would rather be here with me than over there."

Rodrick's eyes jumped back and forth as he read the sentences on her small screen. Then he suddenly thrust the phone back to her and shoved her out his way, rushing out of the apartment.

Quita Wheeler sighed and flopped down on the bed. *Damn*, she thought. *Maybe I shouldn't have showed his ass that status after all.*

Tyesha816: Thank you to everybody that showed up to my baby girl's fourth birthday party! She had a great time! Just about everybody she wanted to show up, showed up. Thank you guys!—at *Great Wolf Lodge.*

August 13th, 6:45 p.m.

CHAPTER 2

One of Rodrick's closest friends, Gideon Byers, helped me and my best friend, Deja Michelle, put all the gifts in the trunk of my Pontiac G6. I gave them both hugs.

"Thank you, guys," I said.

"No problem," said Gideon. "I'll follow you to the crib and help you unload if you want me to."

"I think I got it."

Deja was holding my daughter, Kylie, on her thick hips. She said, "You should let him help you since you-know-who isn't here to do it."

Gideon added, "I don't mind at all."

It was funny to me how two people that hung together could be so different. Gideon was kindhearted and treated people with respect. Rodrick was an arrogant asshole who cared more about hoes in the streets than his own daughter. I never would have thought he would have missed his daughter's first birthday since he'd been out of prison.

"I'll give you gas money for going out of your way," I said to Gideon.

"Gas money?" He laughed me off.

He shut the trunk of my car for me, and when Deja let my daughter down I thought I heard her whisper something to Gideon. I always wondered about them two. They claimed they weren't seeing each other but it always seemed like they were conspiring every time they got around each other. And they both were very beautiful people, so I wouldn't be surprised if they were creeping. Gideon and Deja both had light complexions—about the same tone as me, I guess—and their bodies were banging! Deja came a long way since high school; I'm talking at least a 100 pounds. Looking at her now in her tiny red bikini, she was thick in the right places, and the loss of weight brought out the cheek bones that had been hiding. As far as Gideon's looks, this was actually the first time I had seen him with his shirt off. He was tall and medium built with real defined abs. His eyes were a light gray—and no they weren't contacts; I checked. When I saw them playing with Kylie together in the pool, I thought, *Aww, what a cute couple.* It probably was only a matter of time before they had their own baby.

Deja told me she'd talk to me later. Gideon held my door open for me and I thanked him as I slid in the driver's seat.

"You remember how to get to my house?" I asked.

"Yeah. I get off on 63rd, right?"

"Uh-huh. Just follow me. I don't drive fast."

Suddenly, a Dodge Challenger with custom blue lights pulled up in front of my car and stopped with a *screech.* Rodrick got out, and the first person he said something to was Gideon. He gave him dap and joked that Gideon was dressed like a surfer in his board shorts and thong sandals.

"Glad you're in a good mood," I said to him. "Why'd you finally decide to show up? You saw my status update?"

Rodrick played dumb. "What status update? I came to wish my daughter a happy birthday."

"Daddy!" Kylie cheered from the backseat.

He opened the back door and left her buckled in as he tickled her neck and gave her a kiss on the cheek. Then he reached in his pocket and pulled out a stack of twenties—with the currency band still attached—and handed it to her. I looked at him like he was crazy. What was a four-year-old supposed to do with a thousand dollars cash?

"Happy Birthday," he said to her.

"Thank you, Daddy."

He pulled out his phone and snapped a picture of her holding the cash. Then he looked at me as if he expected a "thank you" from me too.

"Seriously?" I said to him in disbelief. "You forgot about her birthday, didn't buy her a gift, so you give her a stack of money? How thoughtful."

"I didn't forget about her birthday. You didn't call me and tell me you changed the venue."

"I shouldn't have had to call you," I shot back. "I posted it on my events page last week. How come Gideon knew where and when it was and you didn't, and he doesn't even have a Site page?"

"I don't be on it like that."

"Shut up, you make more posts in a day than me."

"No, I don't."

"Yes, you do. And all yo little ho friends always leave a comment. You was probably over that Angela youngandfly Serrano's house. Or probably one of the other many hoes that Likes yo statuses all the time."

"This is what I gotta deal wit'," Rodrick said to Gideon. "I need to be like you and go without having a Site page."

"No, you need to be like him and show up to yo daughter's party," I countered. "She was asking where you were the whole time."

Rodrick was playing me off again. I heard him ask Gideon why he didn't call him. Gideon shrugged and said he would have but he left his phone in his pocket when he jumped in the pool. That was half true; Gideon was actually about to call him before he got his phone wet. I took the phone from him so he couldn't call, told him if Rodrick couldn't remember to show up on his own, then he didn't deserve to come.

17

When I heard Rodrick say something to him about drugs, I turned my head. I didn't want to hear anything about their dealings. That way if either one of them got indicted, I wouldn't know a thing.

My phone beeped and I pulled it out my purse. I had notifications from my Site page. I tapped the screen with my thumb and saw that 39 people had "Liked" my status update. I clicked on the comments feed and started reading:

> **Christina MsFineGirl:** I had a great time! Thanks for inviting me!
>
> **Atlanta Baby:** I think Kylie liked my gift the most :)
>
> **Rita RealSpit Gibson:** You have a beautiful baby girl. Give her lots of love and never let up.
>
> **Quita Wheeler:** Tell her happy birthday for me.
>
> **Joanne Dunley:** Sorry I couldn't come. Stuart didn't come back with my car in time.

Ladykiller: I wish I was there

I knew everybody on here personally that commented on my post except the Quita Wheeler chick, Rita, and Ladykiller. From her info page, it looked like Quita graduated at the same school and in the same year as Rodrick and a few of my other friends. She'd randomly comment or Like one of my posts, and that was cool. Rita was an older woman in her late 40's who always made inspirational quotes that sometimes gave me that boost I needed. But Ladykiller was something else altogether.

Every time—and I mean *every time*—I made a post, Ladykiller would Like it. He was the true definition of a stalker. There was very little about him on his profile page. All it said was that we went to the same school and graduated the same year. But I didn't remember him. And neither did Deja. He looked handsome in his profile picture—360 waves in his hair, piercing brown eyes, and a cute barely-grown-in mustache. But the question was—was it really his picture?

I showed Rodrick and Gideon my phone. "Look. It's him again. Look what he posted."

They both read it. Rodrick said, "You think it's funny, Tyesha. You need to quit playin' and delete his ass."

I took my phone back. "Delete all of yo groupie stalkers and I'll delete mine."

Tyesha816: At Planet Fitness, gettin' it in like a G is 'sposed ta. LOL!—*with* **Deja Michelle**.

August 14th, 4:13 p.m.

CHAPTER 3

Fifteen minutes in, with five more to go, I jacked my arms back and forth on the elliptical machine. My sports bra was soaked between my breasts from all the sweat running down my neck. It was like my pink headband wasn't working. Still, I kept pumping, with Cash Out's "Drip" playing in one of my eardrums. I left the other earbud hanging against my body so I could listen to Deja preach to me.

"He's gonna keep treating you any kind of way until you dump his ass," said Deja through her heaving pants. She was sweating just as hard as me on the elliptical to my right. "As long as you keep lettin' him play you, he's gonna continue to play you. He's never gonna change."

"Everybody's capable of change. Even gangsters. You see he's changed a lot since he got out of jail this last time. He found God."

"Yeah, but he just uses the Bible to his advantage. He uses it to keep you in check. Whenever you accuse him of cheating, he just spits out a passage about trust. What did he tell you last time? That you were just scared he'd leave you, and God says there's no fear in love. And then you turned around and made that yo status update."

I smiled. "I got a lot of Likes."

"You're always joking. You need to take life more seriously. That's why people always take advantage of you," Deja said sternly. "But I know the real reason you haven't broken up with him yet ..."

"Which is?" I asked.

"You don't want to change yo relationship status to 'single.' You're so caught up by what those internet people think of you. You're too embarrassed to be single. But don't you think him sleeping around on you is more embarrassing? You post all these stats about how much you

26

love him and how much you love being in love, but deep down you're hurting. I can see it, girl."

"So wrong," I said.

Sort of true, I retracted in my head. But I wasn't about to admit it. Total, I'd say I had six years invested in Rodrick Brown. We met in high school, back when I was a 17-year-old junior and he a senior. We had a child together, and everybody in school—even people outside of school, like my mother—expected us or wanted us to fail. I just wanted to prove everybody wrong. Every relationship has its ups and downs. I didn't want to be like the other girls I saw changing their relationship statuses back and forth between "in a relationship" and "single" every other month. That would be beyond embarrassing. If I was going to change my status, I wanted it to go from "in a relationship" to "engaged," and eventually to "married"—in that order. Shame on me for sticking it out with an imperfect man I believe in.

"I'm trying to keep you from being hurt," Deja said. "I see it coming."

"Did you see his status update today?" I asked.

"Yeah, I did. He posted a picture of Kylie holding all that money, talking 'bout, 'My daughter is balling harder than you niggas.' Rodrick is a piece of work."

"Guess who Liked it?"

"Me and about 50 other people."

"Yeah, but I'm talkin' about that girl Angela youngand-fly Serrano. She's stalking him *hard*. It's disrespectful. I know she sees that he's in a relationship. I know she clicked on the link and seen my page. She knows who I am."

"And she doesn't care. Neither does Rodrick. You see he hasn't deleted her. Nine times out of ten he's fuckin' her. Have you ever thought that maybe he likes this girl? Maybe he wants to be with her, but you're holding him back. Maybe he's torn between this girl and the mother of his child."

"Bad theory," I said.

She laughed. "I'm through with you."

I got to my third mile before Deja did, but I kept going until she finished. We were supposed to hit the weights next but she gave an excuse about how she was too tired today. Usually I would get her to stay by giving her the guilt trip—telling her the pounds could crawl back on her hips if she didn't mix in weight lifting with the cardio. But I didn't this time.

I wanted her to leave.

As I sat down on the leg press alone and mounted my feet against the plate, I thought about all the people that wanted to see me and Rodrick fail. The anger helped me to push out an extra three sets. When I stood up, my hamstrings burned so bad I had to pigeon-walk to the showers.

Under the streaming shower head, I examined my body to see if I had any improvements. I tightened my tummy and still saw the same flatness, no six-pack. Turning my leg so my thigh muscles flexed, I thought I saw more definition but it could've just been the gleam of the water playing tricks on me. Sometimes it frustrated me how people new to exercising—like Deja—could start working-out and get better results than somebody that had been doing it way longer. I really think I reached my fitness pique.

When I heard my phone buzz, I leaned halfway out the frosted glass stall and checked it. Somebody else made a comment about my status today. I tapped my screen and read it.

Ladykiller: Which one are you at?

I freaked out. I took my towel and started washing the suds off of me as fast as I could. Was this guy really going to try and meet me here? I suddenly regretted letting Deja leave so easily.

Throwing on my Ruskin Eagles hoodie and campus pants and slinging my gym bag strap over my shoulder, I high-tailed it out of the showers. I could tell I didn't dry off good enough because my booty and my legs still felt wet.

I was almost to the door when I saw a man that resembled Ladykiller's profile picture coming in the building. I stopped so fast I stumbled forward a little.

"Tyesha Fenty," he called with a big smile.

He used my real name, not my Site name. I figured he knew it because most of my relatives on my page had the last name Fenty. He was wearing a black sweat suit with neon green resistance bands slung over his shoulder.

When he opened his arms for a hug, I slightly turned my shoulder toward him so he couldn't get a full embrace.

"How you doing?" he asked, as if we were old buddies.

"I'm good," I said with a nervous smile. "Just got through workin' out. Funny we should meet up here."

"It is, ain't it? I was already on my way here when I saw yo status. I didn't know if you was at this one or the one in Overland Park. You stay near here?"

"No, I stay far, far out. Clear across town." Actually, I stayed right down the street. About six blocks from here. I took a step toward the door, hoping he would get the hint.

"How's yo little girl doing? Kylie, right?"

"She's fine. I have to go pick her up."

"I know. Yo momma's watching her until you find another daycare. Is she getting any better with that hoarding? I remember you posted a status about her problem of not being able to throw anything away."

It felt super weird hearing him mention personal stuff about my family. And I know he could see the uncomfortable look on my face.

"I really have to go," I said. I didn't want to just walk off because that would have been rude.

"I won't hold you up."

I smiled and headed out the door. By the time I got my bag in my trunk and my butt in the driver's seat and checked my phone, Ladykiller had already posted a message on my Site wall.

Ladykiller > Tyesha816: It was good seeing you!

Crazy motherfucker, I thought. I tapped the "settings" icon and quickly clicked on the "block" feature. Now he'd never be able to see my status updates again.

Tyesha816: Hey yall! Be careful what yall put on here. These people is crazy and will stalk you. I'm talking from experience!

August 14th, 5:09 p.m.

CHAPTER 4

I couldn't believe it. Yesterday when I was here at my mother's house, I at least had a pathway to the kitchen. Now, standing in the threshold of the front door, I saw in order to get through the house I'd have to crawl over a bunch of cardboard boxes. She must have gone out and bought more crap.

Most of the boxes were open, with long handles and sharp ends of appliances sticking up out of some of them, which made it that much harder navigating to the kitchen. I bumped my knee on the edge of the end table—the one thing that was supposed to be in the living room—and dropped my phone in a box. When I bent down to pick it up, I saw a chain and a heart-shaped locket stuck between some taxes paperwork.

I pulled it out and held it up. At first I thought it was one of my mother's old charms, until I opened it. I let out a laugh. It was a tiny throwback picture of me and Rodrick inside. Our prom picture. In it, my sideburns were horridly gelled down and Rodrick had a full set of gold teeth.

"Can I give this to Kylie, momma?"

Velma Fenty was in the kitchen chopping up an onion insanely fast into little pieces. She paused mid-chop to look. "And you wonder why I hold on to all this stuff," she said. "There's a lot of memories in some of those boxes."

"I never said you should get rid of all of it. Just go through it and get rid of the stuff you don't need."

"I will."

"You've been saying that for at least twenty years. I remember building club houses in the attic out of your packed boxes. I bet it's a picture of one of my club houses in here somewhere."

I dug in the box and found another picture. It was taken at one of my birthday parties, I don't know which year. The little girl with the glitter all over her face in the bottom corner was me; my face was blurred from running past the camera. The shot of my dad though, holding one of the kids at the party, had good sharpness and contrast. He was captured eternally smiling at my blurry head.

I showed the flick to my mom. "Who is this little boy Daddy is holding? Is that Aunt Jene's son?"

Velma snatched the picture, crumpled it and tossed it in the waste basket.

"Momma!" I whined.

"You want me to start getting rid of stuff. There you go."

"How can you still hate him? He's dead! And I don't have that many pictures of him." I got the photo out the trash and uncrumpled it on the counter.

"Am I supposed to forgive him because he's dead?" she asked.

"Yes!"

"I can't do it, Tyesha. I forgave him too many times and he kept cheating. And I see you making the same mistakes I made. When are you gonna let that no-good boy Rodrick go? Every time I check your profile page, I pray to God your relationship status has changed. I'm disappointed every time."

Sometimes I wished I hadn't added my mother as a friend. I introduced her to the Site about three years ago, not too long after my father, a Rollin 60s Crip who migrated from Los Angeles, died. He burned to death in a pool hall fire. His body was discovered, black and charred, with his arms protectively wrapped around his girlfriend—and that infuriated my mother even more. I got her to create a profile in hopes that she would find a male friend from her high school days, but it seemed like she paid more attention to my stats than her peers'.

"I don't want you to think I'm 'stalking' your page," she went on. "I don't comment on your statuses like I used to. I'm just worried about you, Tyesha."

I realized what she was getting at. "Momma, my status today wasn't about you."

She started chopping again.

"I'm serious. It was about somebody else."

"Okay, whatever. Your daughter's upstairs."

STATUS

In the mail bin beside the microwave, I caught sight of an opened bill with Wells Fargo printed on the return address. I didn't have to read the whole letter to know what it was. Two words at the top said it all: "mortgage" and "foreclosure." In the past, I had tried to give my mother money because I knew she was struggling to make it after my father passed. She refused because she thought it was going to come from Rodrick's drug money. Not that she was against drug money—my father sold drugs from time to time. She was just against *Rodrick's* money. She hated him because we had a child out of wedlock and because, in her eyes, he should be treating me way better.

I gave my mother a warm hug from behind and went up and found Kylie playing with some of my old dolls. I started to ask her where she found them, but it was obvious she'd got them out of one of the many boxes cluttering this room. She loved coming over here because she never knew what she'd find.

After giving her the wettest kisses and hugging her until she grunted for air, I pushed some old clothes off the twin bed and had a seat. Crossing my legs as I loaded up

The Site on my phone, a childish grin spread across my face. I couldn't wait to see the comments about my stalker stat and respond.

Cara Unbroken Fisher: My ex-boyfriend's cousin keep telling me how sexy I am on all the photos I post. Ugh! He is ugly as shit.

Christina MsFineGirl: That's why I'm extra careful who I accept as my friend on here. If u don't know me, DON'T SEND ME A FRIEND REQUEST!

Melissa Nelson: I feel you, Tyesha. My next door neighbor always tells me "good morning" and "good night" on my wall. It wouldn't feel so weird if he wasn't a 54-year-old white man! That's why I keep all my curtains closed.

Quita Wheeler: One of my so-called "friends" came to my job once, trying to mack on me. I played his ass to the left. Get a life, fool.

Tyesha816: @Quita Wheeler. That's what happened to me! A stalker showed up where I work-out at. He tried to make it look like he just so happened to show up at the same time as me. Needless to say, I blocked his ass.

Joanne Dunley: OMG!

Deja Michelle: when was this??!!

Tyesha816: Right after you left.

Fedbound Marley: I love all my stalkers!

When Fedbound Marley's comment popped up, I laughed out loud and Kylie came and looked at my phone to see what was so funny. She saw it was reading involved so she went back to playing with her dolls.

I clicked Like on Marley's post.

Then I scrolled to Rodrick's page to see what was going on with him. At the top of his wall was a message that a guy named Kenneth C.r.e.a.m. posted about six minutes ago. I gasped as I read it. And dark anger began boiling inside me.

Immediately, I dialed his number and put the phone to my ear. It rang until it went to the voicemail. I called two more times and it did the same thing.

I called Gideon.

"Hello?"

"Are you with Rodrick?" I asked.

He hesitated. "Nah, I'm solo."

"I really need to talk to him, Gideon. If he's with you, put him on the phone."

"I'm not with him. I'm serious. But he should be calling me in a couple minutes. What's wrong?"

"When you talk to him, tell him to check his profile page as soon as possible. And after that, tell him I'm through playing his games."

I hung up, tried to squeeze my phone until it broke. I looked up at the ceiling and took a breath, hoping my tears wouldn't fall with my head back. I didn't want to cry in front of Kylie. My instincts were screaming for me to go out in the streets and find Rodrick, give him the biggest ass kicking he ever received. But dinner would be ready soon and I know my mom would be pissed if me and Kylie left before eating.

I deleted the message Kenneth posted on my baby's father's page. The deletion would only effect my profile, though. Everybody on the Web who was friends with them would still be able to see the post, but at least I wouldn't have to.

Kenneth C.r.e.a.m. > Rodrick Al-Bashir:

Stay the fuck away from my baby momma's house, nigga! Or I'ma beat yo ass AGAIN!

August 14th, 5:30 p.m.

CHAPTER 5

Ain't nothin' wrong wit' *lying a little bit on ya status update,* Kenneth Murberry thought, as he read through his comments. *I needed to get my point across.*

The fact was he never beat up Rodrick Brown. But he did push him to the floor years ago in the high school cafeteria, and as Rodrick got to his feet security was there to keep them separated. They'd been arguing about who fucked Wendy Hartley first—who was now Kenneth's baby's momma—and when Rodrick turned and showed pictures of Wendy naked on his phone to everybody in the lunch room, Kenneth shoved him from behind.

He'd tried hard not to post anything on Rodrick's profile. But enough was enough. The last straw was when he saw that Wendy clicked Like on the picture Rodrick uploaded of his daughter holding a stack of cash. He told her to stop commenting and Liking all his shit! It was her fault that he blasted him over the internet.

When his phone started ringing, he took his sweet time before answering.

"What the fuck is yo problem?" Wendy hollered.

"You know what my goddamn problem is. Get off Rodrick's dick. I told yo goofy ass to stay off his fuckin' profile."

"I have!"

"I just saw you Liked the picture of his daughter."

"So what? Everybody Liked it. I haven't been commenting on his statuses like I used to."

"I don't want you Liking his shit either."

"Who the fuck are you to tell me what to do? Take care of yo son and I *might* let you call some shots. And you act like I'm the only one that be Liking people's statuses on The Site. You always comment and Like the same bitches' pictures: Quita Wheeler, Angela youngandfly Serrano, Deja Michelle, Janice Tillot, Tyesha816, Christina Ms-FineGirl ... need I name more? You Like all they pictures but haven't Liked *not one* I've uploaded of yo son. And you talking about me on Rodrick … Did you know Tyesha is Rodrick's baby momma?"

Of course I did.

"But I'm not fuckin' her, though," Kenneth said.

"I'm not fuckin' Rodrick!" Wendy snapped.

"You can't even lie right. I saw yo sister's status, talking about she just got a bag of that Girl Scout Cookie Kush dropped off and she tagged you in the picture. Everybody knows Rodrick is one of the only niggas that sell that strand of weed in Kansas City. And if I'm not mistaken, yo sister still stays wit' you. So I know he was over there."

She sucked her teeth. "Just because somebody drops off some weed don't mean I let him in. You better delete yo status before he sees it. I know you're just trying to get attention. But you're barking up the wrong tree."

"Bitch, I am the tree."

Kenneth hung up on her. *Delete my status? Yeah, right.*

Flicking his thumb against his screen, he scrolled down to the newest comments on his post.

Smitty Down4Whatever: LMAO! You a fool, bro!

Mitch tiredofballin Walker: If he didn't get the picture before, I bet he do now! LOL!

Ed Capone: Don't trip on that fuck nigga.

Kenneth C.r.e.a.m.: @Ed Capone--> Sometimes you gotta go on these niggas. They think just because they got a name and some money that gives them the right to fuck every bitch. But not mine, pussy muthafucka!

Ed Capone: I heard that. I already know you gone hog him out like you did in high school.

Kenneth C.r.e.a.m.: Nah. I let him off easy then. This time I'ma springboard clothesline his ass.

Ed Capone: LOL!

Kenneth C.r.e.a.m.: R U coming through?

Ed Capone: Yeah, as soon as my momma get back. You at the house, right?

Kenneth C.r.e.a.m.: Where else I'ma be?

STATUS

Kenneth scanned through his newsfeed while he waited for Ed to show up. He saw Tyesha's status about stalkers and his eyebrows furrowed. *Was she talking about me?* he wondered. He had liked a few of her photos and commented on six or seven over the last couple of weeks but definitely not enough activity on her page to be labeled a stalker. Right? He wasn't about to give himself a headache thinking about it. Women were crazy. *If you Liked their statuses, you were a stalker; if you didn't, you were a hater.*

He hoped she saw his message he posted on Rodrick's wall. That would surely get her juices going. If everything panned out like he wanted it to, her relationship status would revert back to "single," and he'd post LMAO's in Rodrick's inbox for a week. Even though Kenneth had won Wendy in high school, he had always felt like Rodrick one-upped him by getting Tyesha Fenty pregnant. Tyesha was one of the sexiest—if not *the* sexiest—females in their graduating class.

Laying back on the couch and kicking his feet up on the arm rest, he scrolled through Tyesha's endless photos to see if there were any new ones he hadn't seen yet.

Until there was a knock at his door.

He looked through the peep hole and was startled by Ed's fish eye. "Nigga, don't scare me like that," he said, as he flung the door open.

Ed suddenly lunged into him involuntarily, as Rodrick gripped him by the collar with a third generation Glock 17 pressed to his head.

"Hands up, neighbor!" Rodrick barked at Kenneth.

But in a state of panic, Kenneth turned and fled through his house, scraping his elbow against the wall as he pushed himself towards the back door. He slammed against it, then yanked it open.

His heart jumped when he saw Gideon standing in his backyard with an M4 Carbine braced expertly against his shoulder, the 14-inch chrome-moly steel barrel aimed dead at Kenneth's chest. Submitting, Kenneth slowly put his hands behind his head, as Gideon stepped into the house and shoved him back further into the kitchen. He sat Kenneth down at the table where Rodrick had Ed hostage.

"I'm sorry," Kenneth pleaded. "I'll delete that shit. I was just talkin' shit. I didn't mean no disrespect."

"I just got here," Ed moaned pitifully. "I don't even know what I did."

They both watched as Rodrick, clad in black open-knuckle gloves, set a brown paper bag on the table that gave off a greasy scent of fast food. He opened up the cabinet and got out several cups and filled them with ice water. Then he pulled out a chair and sat, reaching in the greasy bag and pulling out a few chili dog burgers. He distributed them evenly.

"You eatin' with us?" he asked Gideon, who held the rifle cocked to the ceiling in standby.

"Nah, I'm good, bro. Do yo thang."

Rodrick gently reached his hands across the table and held them there, palms up. Kenneth, trembling uncontrollably, glanced at an even more frightened Ed. They both were confused.

"Give me your hands," Rodrick said.

Hesitantly, Kenneth and Ed placed their hands in Rodrick's.

55

"Would any of you two like to say Grace?"

They both shook their heads no.

"Well, bow your heads," Rodrick said, lowering his chin to his chest and closing his eyes. "Dear Heavenly Father—"

"Close your eyes!" Gideon yelled at them.

They shut them immediately.

"Dear Heavenly Father, I want to thank you for bringing us together without incident or casualty. Please bless Kenneth Murberry and Edward Davis, for they are my enemies. And I ask you to put forgiveness in my heart, oh Lord, and their hearts as well, oh Lord, as we share this meal today. In Jesus name we pray. Amen."

"Amen," Kenneth and Ed said in unison.

"Let's eat," Rodrick said.

Cautiously, the two unwrapped their burgers. Ed licked chili juice off his finger to taste test it. Kenneth didn't even do that much. He stared at his burger blankly, before laying his eyes back on Rodrick. He couldn't figure out how they—

"Pictures," Rodrick said, reading his expression. "From the pictures you uploaded to The Site, especially the one with your house in it, it was easy to find out where you live. I also know from your posts that you and Ed meet up over here every night to drink beer and watch videos online because Ed's internet is cut off. And I just saw your interesting status update about me, which you, Edward, stated that you were on your way over here. I thought I'd come to address some issues. I do homework on all my enemies ... and you and Ed made it easy for me."

"We don't have any issues, Rodrick," said Kenneth. "I just got off the phone with Wendy. She told me she only seen you when you came to drop off some of that fire GSC you sold to her sister. She explained it to me. She told me you weren't even there to see her."

Rodrick bit into his burger, the pickles crunching quietly within his jaws. He swallowed and dabbed his lips with a napkin. "She lied to you," he told Kenneth. "I *am* fuckin' her. I been fuckin' her at least three times a week since I got out of prison. You know that profile picture she just uploaded of herself, the one that's cropped with her kissing the camera? That arm around her shoulder belongs to me. She's a wonderful human being, but with dick-sucking skills that can only be described as extraterrestrial. And if you think I'ma give that up, you're sadly mistaken."

Kenneth blinked. He had misjudged Rodrick completely. From some of Rodrick's status updates about Christ and the Holy Spirit, he thought Rodrick had come out of jail on a church kick, like some of his other homeboys he knew that left the streets alone. He'd hoped Rodrick wouldn't think twice about the message he posted on his wall. But it was becoming clear that Rodrick was spiritually fucked up.

"Uh … well …" Kenneth stammered. "If yall like each other, that's coo' wit' me, bro. I apologize. I'll delete that shit I posted immediately."

"Give me your phone," Rodrick said. "I'll do it for you."

Kenneth handed over his cell phone, but as soon as it left his fingertips, a thought suddenly occurred to him. "Wait a minute! Give it back so I—"

But Rodrick already had the screen unlocked. Rodrick's face lit up with rage, and Kenneth skeeted out a spittle of pee in his pants before clenching his bladder tight. Rodrick was staring at the Site profile of his baby's mother, Tyesha Fenty.

"You planning to do harm to my family, too?!" Rodrick boomed.

"I was just looking through her photos, Rodrick! I swear to God!"

Rodrick jumped to his feet and shot Kenneth in the forehead, the bullet's velocity slinging him out the chair onto the floor in a heap. He reached over the table and let off several more shots into his body. "Don't ever use the Lord's name in vain!"

Ed started screaming so loud he covered up his own ears. Terrified, he pressed his body against the wall and continued shrieking with enormous wide eyes. When Rodrick pointed the Glock 17 at him, he somehow opened up his lungs wider into a bloodcurdling holler.

Boom!

Silence.

Rodrick Al-Bashir: "If your enemy is hungry, feed him; if he is thirsty, give him something to drink. In doing this, you will heap burning coals—or hot lead!—on his head."
Romans 12:20

August 15th, 2:39 a.m.

CHAPTER 6

Close to one o'clock in the afternoon, the lobby of the Missouri Department of Motor Vehicles was near empty. It was probably the rain, I guessed, pouring down in sheets outside that kept customers from showing up. This was rare. I hardly ever had a chance to check my phone for messages at this time of day.

Standing at my counter with my phone hidden, I logged in to The Site and saw that 66 people had Liked Rodrick's status. He had some Bible verse on there that talked about enemies. I probably should have made that post myself and tagged him in it, because how he treated me—coupled with the things I did for him—was like me feeding my enemy. Last night he called me back trying to explain himself. He denied sleeping with that guy Kenneth C.r.e.a.m.'s baby's mother, said he was just hating on him like he'd been doing since high school. I told him how I felt, and how embarrassed I was. Then I did the dumbest thing ever—I let him come over … and I let him fuck me senseless. I had hopes to cook breakfast for him and Kylie this morning—*I know Kylie would have loved eating breakfast with her daddy*—but he was gone when I rolled over this morning and felt the empty side of the bed.

He couldn't even stay long enough for breakfast.

My notification icon was lit so I clicked on it. I sucked my teeth when I saw a friend request from Ladykiller. Clicking "ignore," I went to my newsfeed to see what people were getting into this weekend. As I scrolled through, I started to see a grave pattern.

Joanne Dunley: Rest in peace.

Mitch tiredofballin Walker: R.I.P my niggas

Rita RealSpit Gibson: Two people's lives were lost last night. I don't and probably will never know the real circumstances behind their deaths, but they both will be in my prayers.

Smitty Down4Whatever: R.I.P. Kenneth "C.r.e.a.m." Murberry and Edward Young. We lost two real niggas.

Christina MsFineGirl: I don't understand why the police never catch these people.

Janice Tillot: @Christina MsFineGirl. The police have leads. They said one of his Site friends is a suspect.

Monica I'mProbably Wright: They could be right next to us in the grocery store. It's scary. That's why I'm moving away from Kansas City as soon as I can.

Wendy 'youlovetotaste' Hartley: Stay out of my inbox! Just because Kenneth was my baby daddy don't mean I know what happened to him!

"Tyesha, I told you to stay off the phone while you're at your counter."

Ruth Jameson, my supervisor, startled me. I quickly stuffed my phone in my pocket. This wasn't the first time I had been caught using my phone while on the clock.

"I was just checking my e-mails," I lied.

Ruth stared at me icily. "I don't care what you were doing. It's not allowed. And I've told you this for the umpteenth time. Do you want this job?"

"Yeah, I do. I'm sorry."

"It doesn't seem like it."

"I do. I'll stay off my phone, Ruth. I'm sorry."

Ruth held her palm out. "Give me the phone, Tyesha."

The most absurd expression appeared on my face. "Give you my phone? I'm not giving you my phone? I'm 22 years old. I'm not a child."

"The people in my office told me to get any electronic devices from you," Ruth said.

"What people?"

"Detectives. They're in there waiting on you."

I glanced at her palm. "Are you serious? What do they want?"

"They wouldn't tell me. They just told me to get your phone before I sent you in. Is that the only thing electronic on you?"

I started to walk away when Ruth grabbed my arm. I shrugged her off. "Don't touch me, Ruth. I'm not giving you my phone. I know my rights."

Nervous wasn't the word. I brushed the thighs of my skirt and buttoned the second button from the top on my white and violet pocket-front blouse, trying to look as presentable as possible, as I walked down to Ruth's office. I patted my hair and wondered, *Do I look guilty?* My heart felt like it was about to explode.

When I walked into Ruth's office, one of the two detectives told me to shut the door and have a seat. They were both Black men, and they had on casual clothes. If Ruth hadn't told me ahead of time, I probably wouldn't have known they were detectives.

"My names Detective Frisk," said the one that was sitting down behind Ruth's desk. The other detective was perched on the edge of it. He wore a close-fitted gray tee that hugged his toned muscles, with black and gray Nike

Shox on his feet. "And this is my partner, Detective Co-peland."

Copeland was closest to me and extended his hand. I shook it.

"I know my rights," I said. "And I don't have to give you my phone if I don't want to."

Frisk looked confused. "We're not asking you for any of your property. We just have some questions."

I knew it. Ruth just wanted my phone to be an ass.

"We're here to talk to you about an incident that took place last night, roughly around 10:00 p.m.," Frisk said. "Two young men by the names of Edward Young and Kenneth Murberry were murdered and we'd like to know if you had any information to provide us."

I tensed. "I don't. Why would I?"

It was almost as if Detective Copeland had seen my answer coming. He quickly reached in his pocket and pulled out a photo that he laid on the desk in front of me.

"Do you know this man?" he asked.

Of course I did. It was the father of my child, Rodrick Brown. It was a mugshot of him from a couple years ago when he caught a possession of narcotics charge. His dreads hung down his face like tangled black ropes.

Without thinking, I said, "No, I don't know him."

Detective Frisk sighed.

Copeland picked the picture up and held it close to my face. "This isn't your baby daddy?"

"Oh, yeah it is," I retracted. "I didn't recognize the picture. It's a bad photo." I squinted at it. "Yeah, that's him. Yall think he knows something about it?"

"We need to have a chat with him, that's all. He's on our list of people to talk to. Do you know where we can locate him?"

I shook my head no. "I haven't seen him in like a month."

Detective Copeland started biting his bottom lip as if he was irritated.

Leaning forward, balling his hands together in a fist and placing them on the desk, Detective Frisk looked at me hard. "Ms. Fenty, or should I say Tyesha816, we've had a looksee at your Site page. You uploaded a photo of him and your daughter to your page eight days ago.

And on Rodrick's Site page, he uploaded a photo of his daughter holding a large amount of cash on your daughter's birthday. And you're trying to tell me you haven't seen him in a month?"

"I haven't," I said adamantly.

"Let's cut the shit. If you keep lying to us, you can get in some serious trouble. This is a double homicide we're talking about. We already know that Kenneth made a threatening post to Rodrick Brown yesterday that we can't confirm because it was mysteriously deleted. But this morning Rodrick Brown made a post that has raised questions about his culpability in the murders. And we've dialogued with several of your Site friends, and they've told us that he's been known to stay with a lot of women, but mainly with you. Our records stating that he home-planned to your house corroborate that."

"He lived with me when he first got out. That's it. And he's never lived with no other females either. It's a bunch a liars on The Site. Yall are detectives, yall should know that. And I may have uploaded that picture of Rodrick and my daughter recently, but that don't mean it was *taken* recently. I haven't seen him in a while. Maybe it's not been a whole month, but it feels like it."

"We need to know where we can find him," Copeland said.

I asked, "Do I legally have to answer any more questions?"

"Not at this moment, no. But if you're called before the court, yes, you *will*," Frisk emphasized. "What we're trying to do is avoid involving you in the whole court process entirely. We'd hate for both the father and mother of your daughter, Kylie, to end up in jail. I'm being real wit' you here."

This didn't feel *real* at all. I was being threatened with jail time and the unimaginable—losing my child. I was surprised they hadn't brought up Gideon. *If it was murder involved, they must have been together, right?* Maybe it was because Gideon didn't have a Site page, and thus the detectives had no idea who he was.

"Tell us what you're thinking," said Frisk.

I looked at both detectives. "No comment," I said.

71

***

As soon as it was time for me to clock out, I raced outside to my car. The rain poured down on me as I fished my phone out and called Rodrick. I had him on the line when I opened my door and slid in the dry driver's seat.

"Hello?"

"Rodrick, detectives just came up to my job looking for you!"

"Did you tell them anything?"

"No, baby. I didn't give them shit. They tried to threaten me but I wasn't going for it," I told him excitedly. I don't know what it was. Whenever I got a chance to take up for Rodrick or protect him, my adrenaline would get going. "They was mad at me when I left that office. I don't know what's gonna happen."

"Good job, baby."

"What are you gonna do?" I asked.

"God told me to turn myself in."

"What?!"

"Look, Tyesha. Everything's gonna work itself out. I've been seeing what people have posted on The Site and the assumptions and threats they're making. I'm not worrying about it and neither should you. It's in God's hands. But as a precautionary measure, I'ma have Gideon come through your house and chill till I get released. Just to be on the safe side."

"What if you don't get released? You're on parole, Rodrick. You could get violated. And you know your parole officer is an asshole."

"I hope I'll be in and out before my parole officer gets word. With God, all things are possible."

I told him I loved him and told him to be careful and I hung up. I wondered what he was talking about when he said "threats." I thumbed my screen and loaded up The Site again when there was a hard knock on my driver's side window.

Startled me good. And when I looked out into the rain, I saw Ladykiller with a hood pulled over his head.

"Shit!" I screamed. I was frozen in fear.

He held his hands up and mouthed "it's just me." Then he gestured for me to roll my window down.

I turned my key—*I didn't start it; I was too scared to*— just to trigger the car's battery. Then I eased the window down halfway. The rain was loud and sprinkles bounced off his hood onto my arm.

"Wussup, Tyesha? I thought that was you sitting in this Pontiac. I recognized it from the photo you put up when you first bought it."

"How did you know I work here?"

"You work here?" He laughed. "Damn, I didn't know that. I just came to get my car tagged up."

"I have to go."

His expression changed. "You had to go last time."

"It's raining. And you're gettin' it in my car."

"Oh, sorry. Well, I'll talk to you later. But before I forget, I saw that you might have accidentally unfriended me on The Site. It might've been a virus or something. I tried to send you another friend request but you haven't accepted it yet. Have you been checking your notifications?"

"Not really. I could've sworn we were still friends on there. I was wondering why you haven't been commenting on my posts."

"I've been wanting to, trust me."

"I'll add you later," I lied, firing up my engine. "But right now I have to go. Nice seeing you."

"Why later?"

"Huh?"

"Add me now."

"My phone battery is low and it's about to die. I don't want to use the last of my battery loading up The Site."

"Ain't that a car charger hooked up to yo cigarette lighter?"

I glanced at my console. The logo on it was glowing, so I couldn't say it didn't work. *Shit!*

"Add me now," Ladykiller said firmly.

I swallowed. "Okay."

Tyesha816 and **Ladykiller** are now friends

CHAPTER 7

Me and Gideon sat awkwardly in two of my daughter's baby stools. The seats were low, about six inches off the ground. My knees almost touched my chest, and Gideon's knees *were* touching his. I was laughing inside and felt bad for him at the same time.

We both held pink cups full of imaginary vodka, as we watched Kylie open up her toy microwave and pull out a tray of plastic cupcakes.

"It's done, lady and gentleman," said Kylie in a serious yet sweet tone.

I giggled. My daughter was really in character. This was most definitely a result of all the food shows I made her watch with me.

She put plates in front of us and placed two cupcakes on them, then laid small leafs on them too. She stood up straight with her hands behind her back, waiting for us to taste it. Her hair was pulled back into a ponytail, a pink ribbon holding it in place. She was the cutest cook in the world.

"And what am I about to eat, young lady?" asked Gideon.

"Cupcake wit' *s'pinkles* and vanilla icing. I mix it wit' honey and onions and China beans."

"And what's that on the side?" I asked.

"It's a leaf."

"Oh." I expected her to make up a fancy edible name for the leaf. I smiled, feeling stupid. "A leaf, right. Nice presentation."

And then there was a quick beep that came from my pocket. It was the sound my phone made when I had a notification from The Site. As soon as I reached in my pocket, my daughter stopped me.

"No, Momma," Kylie whined. "You said you would play wit' me and not get on *ta* Site."

"It might be something important, baby."

"More important *tan* me?"

Nothing was more important than my daughter, but if the threats I had been reading on The Site held any weight, me and her could be in real danger. Since I got off work, about five people—relatives of Kenneth and Ed—had posted in my inbox, threatening to harm Rodrick or me if I didn't cooperate with the police. One of Kenneth's younger cousins simply posted, "Bang! Bang!" Gideon told me not to take any of the messages seriously. He said people who hurled threats online never followed through. I wasn't so sure.

Gideon brought me out of my thoughts. "Honor your promise," he said to me.

I took a deep breath and exhaled. Maybe it was just some spam or a creepy post from Ladykiller. I could check it later.

I took my hand out my pocket and showed my daughter my palm. "No phone, as promised," I said. Gently, I picked up one of the cupcakes and brought it to my lips, then took a bite of the air as if I actually bit into the cake. Chewing, I said, "I can taste the honey. Good job."

Kylie didn't smile. She simply nodded. Like a real chef.

My legs started to cramp so I stretched them out. My phone beeped again and my heart actually began to thump a little faster. It was anxiety. I couldn't remember the last time I'd went this long without checking my profile page, other than when I was asleep. For the next half hour, as me and Gideon helped my daughter make a beaded necklace out of candy, I kept touching my thigh out of habit, feeling for my phone but immediately pulling away to keep my promise.

No phone, I kept reminding myself.

Gideon clutched his stomach. "I think those cupcakes are running through me," he said.

I giggled.

"You know where the bathroom is," I stated.

He nodded, and scurried with a doubled over posture to the rest room.

"I put extra honey in his," Kylie whispered to me.

"Why?"

"So he get sick," she said.

My mouth hung open. I was amused *and* confused.

"Why would you want him to get sick?"

"'Cause he likes you."

I started to ask her where she would get an idea like that, when I thought I heard a light tap on my front door. It was almost 11 o' clock at night and I wasn't expecting anybody. I went in the living room and got Gideon's Walther .380 out his jacket. I clutched the black synthetic grip and jacked the hammer back.

"Who is it?" I asked through the front door.

Nobody answered me.

I opened the door slightly and peeked out. The wind whistled and I could hear the rain pelting against the concrete.

"Anybody?" Gideon asked from behind.

"Nope. I thought I heard something, though." I shut the door. "It sounded like a tap."

"Ain't nobody about to come get you," he said. I handed him his gun and he inspected it. "You actually put a round in it?"

"I don't play about my daughter."

"You know Rodrick just sent me here as a precaution, right? He thinks people think all these twisted thoughts just like him. If he had an enemy, he'd get whoever's close to that enemy, like a family member. But people don't think like that in real life. And if they do, they'd never actually follow through with those thoughts like him. Rodrick is crazy."

"Amen to that."

We had a seat on the couch and I asked him how he and Rodrick became friends—I had always wondered how they met because they were different in so many ways. I knew they met in prison, but that was the extent of it. He told me it was just by chance. They put Rodrick in a cell with him and in the beginning they barely said two words to each other. Over time, they started cooking meals together to save on money and found out that they both had an interest in the financial shows on CNBC. He noticed

Rodrick becoming more fanatical about religion, trying to pressure him to read the Word with him and they started to get into arguments. Gideon was a believer, but not nearly as zealous. Rodrick decided to switch cells but they still had a mutual respect for one another. They promised to stay in touch upon release.

I wanted to hear more. I loved prison stories! I asked him what he was locked up for; Rodrick told me felons didn't like being asked that question but I didn't give a shit. I wanted to know.

Gideon hesitated. He seemed to be pondering where to start. "I killed my wife," he said.

I gasped.

"Nah, I'm just playing," he said, laughing.

"OMG! You had me." I shoved him playfully. "Were you ever married, though?"

"Never."

Lightning flashed outside and the thunder followed, *booming* over the entire house. The lights flicked off and on, off and on. Twice.

"Let me put Kylie to bed," I told him.

***

After the second thunder blast, the lights went off and stayed off for good. Me and Gideon bumped into each other three times trying to find candles. We got three lit and placed them on the coffee table as we lounged on the couch in semi-darkness, getting to know one another.

"I'm not addicted," I said. "Addicted is a strong word."

"What would you call it?" he asked.

"Obsessed."

He laughed. "And that's better?"

"Technically? Yes. If I was addicted, I wouldn't be able to stop. I'd be sucking nutballs for internet access. I'm just *obsessed* with it. And I don't even think I'm as obsessed as most people. I don't post every minute on the hour. For the most part, I post three times a day—when I wake up, then sometime in the afternoon, and at night. Unless it's something super important I have to post, I try to limit 'em to three a day."

"That sounds like a lot to me."

"Trust, it's not," I said. "Why don't you have a profile page? You got something to hide?"

"Nah, that ain't it. I just don't want my business out there like that. That's why I don't understand this social media craze. What happened to a little mystery? Say, hypothetically, I was attracted to you and wanted to get to know you." He put his arm around me. "All I would have to do is go to yo profile page and click on 'info' and there it is. There'd be nothing to learn or discover about you. What once was shared between two people trying to build an intimate relationship is now open for the world to see."

"But ..." I pointed out, "... that can be considered a good thing. You already know enough about me by checking my profile to see if you like me or not. It eliminates people wasting their time. It's impossible to put *everything* about yourself in a post, or even in a thousand posts. There are little things, little nuances and idiosyncrasies, that you don't even know about yourself that your special someone will have to find out—good and bad. Your profile page is just a foundation, a snidbit of you, a starting point to even consider somebody. We need that nowadays.

87

But niggas like you"—I poked him in the chest—"that don't have a profile, ol' off-the-grid-ass niggas, are high risk. What's the real reason behind this off-the-grid-ness? Are you hiding a shameful character that would eventually come out if you made status updates? Does your life suck that bad that you don't have anything to post about? Can you not afford internet?"

"I'm balling," Gideon said. "And my whole life is full of swag."

I laughed. "Not you. I'm just saying."

The candles flickered, and for a second I thought they were going to go out.

"The only downside to it—and I have to admit—is the stalkers. I don't want to start on how many niggas be in my inbox, even though they see I'm in a relationship with Rodrick."

"You can't blame them, though. You're sexy to death. How you gon' be mad at them when that's the basis of social media—connecting with good people, beautiful people. You got a good spirit too, and I know that comes across in your posts. I'm sure you be uploading pictures of your daughter and niggas is seeing the love you have for ya child, knowing if they were to have a child by you, theirs would get the same love. If I had a page, it'd be hard for me not to live in yo inbox. I'd be messaging you every five minutes until you respond. So I'm sure it's hard on these brothas that wanna get at you, knowing you're only a click away."

I blushed. But with it being so dark, I knew he didn't notice. I started biting my clear-coated pinky nail, smiling at how good his words felt. Deep down I knew I was a good woman, but I had wondered if anybody was paying attention. I knew Rodrick wasn't.

Suddenly, Gideon pulled on my wrist and popped my fingernail out of my mouth—and replaced it with his lips.

Magically, the candle lights fluttered out.

His lips consumed mines, nearly sucking all the juice out. I placed my palm against his chest with just enough pressure to let him know I didn't want this.

"What?" he asked breathlessly.

"Gideon, I'm sorry. I'm with Rodrick. I can't do this to him."

"He does it to you."

"I don't care. I'm not that type of girl."

He cleared his throat and gave me some space. "I know
… yeah, I know … and my apologies. I misread some
signs or somethin'. My internal GPS must've malfunc-
tioned."

"It's okay," I said. "And I won't tell Rodrick."

"I wouldn't care if you did."

It was awkward for a minute or so in the total darkness.
Then I told him he was welcome to stay up and watch TV
on my iPad if he wanted. I found it in my bedroom and
brought it to him; it cast a bright white glow of light on his
face that made him squint.

"Thank you for staying here to protect me," I said.

"Any time," he responded dully.

I went up to my room and closed the door.

Laying on my bed, I thought about what just happened.
Fact: my baby's daddy's friend just kissed me. Fact: I have
no idea where that came from. Fact: he was a good kisser.
Or was that an opinion?

My mind was racing and I ran my fingers through my hair. He tried to eat my face! It was funny and so fucked up at the same time. I knew I did the right thing by pushing him away. I was in a relationship with Rodrick—as unstable as it may be, but still officially committed per The Site—and there was a strong possibility that Gideon and Deja were secretly messing around.

Out of curiosity, I pulled out my phone and went to the Missouri DOC website and typed in Gideon Byers' name. He said he was joking about being locked up for killing his wife but I just wanted to be sure. When his face popped up, I gasped. He had a beard in his mugshot, and braids—two characteristics I wasn't that fond of in men. He definitely cleaned himself up since he'd been released.

When I scrolled down to his charges, I saw one count of trafficking drugs, two counts of narcotics possession, and one count of unlawful use of a weapon. No murder charges.

Angela youngandfly Serrano: my boo
kept me safe through the storm last night.
XOXO—*with* **Rodrick Al-Bashir.**

August 16th, 8:45 a.m.

CHAPTER 8

The lights were back on in the morning. My phone was dead so I hooked it up to the wall charger and let it build up. On my way to Kylie's room, I heard two men downstairs laughing. I peeked in on my sleeping baby girl, then trotted down the steps.

"Rodrick, when did you get here?" I asked.

"A few minutes ago," he said. He gave me a hug and a kiss. "The Lord brought me home."

"I see. Hopefully the Lord will keep you home."

"We can only hope. One only knows what He has in store for me."

I glanced at Gideon. He hadn't looked at me at all. "Good morning, Gideon."

"Good morning," he said dryly.

He's still upset with me, I thought. But hopefully he would come back around and we'd have the same relationship before the attempted kiss. I would continue to be nice to him and respect him like I always had.

As I plopped down in between them on the couch, Rodrick told me they didn't charge him with anything. The detectives just asked him questions for a few hours and made him sit in a holding cell even longer. Even though they let him go, he still wasn't out of the water. He said they could still charge him later on down the line if they discovered any new evidence. All they had now was internet speculation and the last comment Kenneth Murberry posted on Rodrick's wall before he was murdered.

My gut feeling told me that he and Gideon were responsible. But one thing I didn't do was ask questions. *I didn't want to know anything and I didn't want to see anything either.*

"Then there's still a chance my parole officer can violate me for coming in contact with the police," Rodrick said. "That's if he finds out. I'll have to go back and finish off the rest of my time. But I'm not gon' worry about it. I already put it in God's hands."

"How much time you got left on your sentence?" I asked him.

"Seven months," Rodrick said.

"That's not that bad. What about you, Gideon? Are you still on parole?"

"Yeah," Gideon replied. "But I'll be done with it in two more days."

"Damn, that's good. Are you gonna celebrate?"

He nodded. "I already got something planned."

"Tyesha, go get dressed," Rodrick said to me. "And while you up there, wake up my baby girl. We're all going out on this beautiful Saturday morning to eat a nice breakfast at the Isle of Capri. Maybe splash a little bit on the crap table too. My treat. It's not often I get to do somethin' nice for the ones I love. I try to show my appreciation as much as I can."

Gideon gave him dap and I one-arm hugged him before racing up the steps. It was times like these that reminded

me why I fell in love with Rodrick. He was so appreciative and generous. Whenever he tried to give me large
amounts of cash, though, I would turn it down or do one
of two things: put it up for his daughter's college tuition,
or put it up for him in case he got incarcerated again. I
didn't want to become dependent on his drug money. But
him taking me and Kylie out was something different.

I was flipping through the hangers of clothes in my
closet when I heard my phone beep. I picked it up and
unlocked the screen, saw a notification lit up on The Site.
When I clicked it, a message appeared alerting me that
someone had posted on Rodrick's wall. I had my settings
set so all Rodrick's interactions on The Site would auto-
matically pop up in my newsfeed, and if someone commented or left a message on his wall, my phone would
beep. Rodrick was a goodhearted person, but I still had to
keep tabs on him.

My phone buffered for a moment, and then the message appeared.

It felt like I got shot in the stomach with a semi-auto-
matic; it was twisting in painful knots as I read the mes-

sage and the time it was posted. I was beyond stunned, woozy almost. I read Angela youngandfly Serrano's comment again, as my feet traveled on their own back downstairs. Before I knew it, I had Rodrick in a deathly chokehold.

"You trifling-ass nigga!" I screamed.

He choked and gagged, trying to wrest my arms from around his neck. As he tried to pull away, he dragged me across the couch but I still stayed latched. I bit into his temple ragefully.

He slammed me over his shoulder onto the carpet.

Gideon pushed him. "Ay, nigga, don't hurt her!"

Rodrick held the side of his face as he maintained his balance. He had minor bleeding. "I'm sorry," he said.

I didn't know if he was apologizing to me or Gideon. I got up and seized two handfuls of his dreads, yanking him around. He slammed into the flatscreen, as I yanked left and he tripped over the coffee table, fell onto it—but not through it.

"You were with that bitch last night!" I hollered. "You fuckin' liar! You weren't locked up!"

"Tyesha, let him go," Gideon said, pulling me by the waist.

"No!! I'ma kill his bitch ass!"

I dragged him off the table and Gideon fell behind me and I fell on top of him. Rodrick got up and ran around the couch. I got up and tried to go after him but Gideon was holding me by the waist again. I threw elbows but he wouldn't let me go.

"What did I do?" Rodrick asked.

"You know what you did, bitch!" I yelled. "Where the fuck were you last night?!"

"I was in jail."

"No, you weren't! You were at that bitch Angela youngandfly Serrano's house!"

"No, I wasn't, Tyesha. I got my release paperwork in my pocket."

"You fuckin' lying bitch! She posted on your wall this morning that you were at her house all fuckin' night! When your daughter is here in the dark with no damn power!"

He blinked guiltily. "She posted what?"

I struggled with Gideon. "Let me go! I'ma murder his bitch-ass!"

"I really was locked up, Tyesha. She just bonded me out, that's all. I tried to call you but your phone was off."

"Let me go, Gideon!"

"Gideon, hold her until I get outside." Rodrick started backpedalling out the door. "A'ight, bro?"

When Rodrick shut the door behind him, Gideon let me go. I ran to the door and yanked it open, dashed down the steps as Rodrick screeched away from the curb. His Challenger screamed down the road.

"I'ma kill his ass," I said to Gideon when I got back in the house. "Can I use your gun?"

"Tyesha, you act like you didn't see this coming," he said.

"Did you know? Were you in on it too? Did he tell you to watch me so I wouldn't be asking where he was?"

"I was played too. He knew I wouldn't do nothing like that to you willingly."

"Can you leave, please?"

"Tyesha, I *swear* I didn't know where he was," Gideon stressed.

"Still, can you leave? Please?"

His jaws clenched, then he threw on his track jacket and strolled out the door.

I sat on the arm of my couch and crossed my arms. Tears slowly fell down my cheeks as I thought of how many people saw Angela youngandfly Serrano's post. Hundreds, maybe thousands. It was bad enough having a man who cheated on me, but for it to be broadcasted over the World Wide Web was literally unbearable. My chest began to constrict on its own, and I found myself trying to catch my breath. It sounded so simple to just change my relationship status and delete Rodrick as a friend, but it wasn't. People would see me as a quitter. And I know for a fact once his status changed, tons of bitches would pounce on him, and Kylie would end up with who knows how many brothers and sisters. But the fight for his love was tormenting my soul.

Then I heard a phone beep.

Wiping my eyes, I pulled my cell out and checked the display. No notifications. Puzzled, I looked over my shoulder and on the couch was a cell phone one of them dropped. I picked it up and unlocked the screen with a quick swipe. It was Rodrick's phone.

I didn't hesitate to log into The Site through his account and check his private messages. I clicked on the exchange between him and Angela that took place exactly 47 minutes ago.

Angela youngandfly Serrano: fuck and run? I see how u do.

Rodrick Al-Bashir: I gotta head over my BMs house and relieve Gideon of his duties.

Angela youngandfly Serrano: I'm getting fed up with u still fucking w/ her

Rodrick Al-Bashir: That's the mother of my child. I'ma always have to fuck with her.

Angela youngandfly Serrano: bull shit just go ur separate ways and pay ur child support. If u want me to pay it for u I will.

Rodrick Al-Bashir: I'm not on child support. And you know I ain't that type of nigga anyway. God rewarded me with my daughter. I can't turn my back on a blessing.

Angela youngandfly Serrano: i won't let u keep using God as an excuse to play me! either u gonna change ur relationship status w/ her or I'm done. U told me if I came to pick u up from the jail last night you would change it.

Angela youngandfly Serrano: hello???!!!

Rodrick Al-Bashir: Sorry. I had to stop texting and driving. I just pulled up to my BMs house.

Angela youngandfly Serrano: answer my question. R u gonna change your status?

Rodrick Al-Bashir: Let's talk about it tonight. You coming to the club, right?

Angela youngandfly Serrano: I'll be there. and ur gonna give me an answer, nigga! count on that!

Angela youngandfly Serrano: did u see
my status update? I tagged u in it I told u I'm
not playing.

Angela youngandfly Serrano: R u still at
ur BM house?

If they thought they were going to meet up and laugh
at me and have fun and dance the night away, they had
another thing coming. I shot to my feet and stormed up
the steps. As I searched through my closet for an outfit
that would hold up good in a fight, I dialed a number on
my phone and put it up to my ear. I had my mother on the
line in no time.

"Hello?" she answered.

"Momma, I need two big favors from you tonight," I
said.

Tyesha816: I might catch a case tonight.

August 16th, 10:10 p.m.

CHAPTER 9

Strobe lights flickered down on me and the dancers and drinkers, giving just enough light to tease my eye with a glimpse of someone's face, but not enough to see that many facial features. Thus, I was having a hard time finding Angela youngandfly Serrano amongst all these people. I had the girl's face etched in my memory from constant webpage visits, but just when I thought I saw an Angela look-a-like, the overhead lights would stream in another direction.

And Travis Porter's "Pussy Real Good" pounding relentlessly out the club speakers kept everybody moving and turning around and away from my line of sight.

Bumping into people on the dance floor, I made my way to the bar and ordered myself a drink. My nerves were bothering me bad. Would I actually swing on this bitch when I saw her? Was Rodrick really worth it? Last time I got into a fight over him, I ended up with a year probation.

Before I let doubt creep all the way in, I threw back a shot of Ciroc and ordered another. Then I felt someone beside me tap the top of my hand.

I turned.

"Whatchu doin' here?" the brotha asked, staring at me from behind black D&G shades.

"Do I know you?"

He lifted up his shades and showed me his deep set brown eyes. They were all I needed to see. "Marley!" I beamed, leaning in and hugging him.

Since grade school, me and Marley Dubois—aka Fed-bound Marley—had been friends. Same middle school, same high school too. I could remember times when he'd get kicked out of class for cracking jokes on teachers. I kept up with his status updates whenever I needed a good laugh. According to the pictures and statuses he posted, he was having a hard time selling drugs. He would post things like, "Somebody stole my scale," and "This weed is bunk but I'ma still try to get it off though." He was the most unsuccessful thug I knew.

I hadn't seen him in I don't know how long, but we sort of stayed in touch through The Site.

"How you doin'?" he asked. "I ain't seen you in years."

"I'm doing okay. How about you?"

"Just tryna stay on my feet. I'm here tryna get these sacks off so I can get my Netflix cut back on."

I laughed a little. I couldn't believe that much came out of me, considering how mad I was. Probably the liquor opening me up.

"You're still a nut. You haven't changed."

"Nope. No reason to. But neither have you, apparently. Lookin' mighty fly tonight," he noted. "I can't tell you how many old females I done ran into that's lookin' like zombies now. High-five."

I sucked my teeth at him, but gave him a high-five. I had on a pair of tight denim jeans and flats. The only thing that could be considered sexy was my top—it was a cascading knit tee with tribal embroidery around the neckline—and my earrings, which were set in crystal fans that pierced my lobes in such a way that couldn't be pulled out.

"Thank you," I said, as I eyed the live crowd around me, searching.

"You sure ain't dressed for jail."

"Huh?"

"The last status update you made. I was like, What the hell? It made me laugh. Talkin' 'bout you gon' catch a case. Not you."

My throat burned when I downed the rest of my second drink. I was thinking about ordering another. Since Marley had seen my recent status, I wondered if he saw the post Angela youngandfly Serrano made on Rodrick's page; if he was friends with either one of them on The Site, then he had. I started to feel warm with embarrassment.

"You got warrants?" Marley asked jokingly.

"No. That status I made didn't mean anything."

"*I* got warrants," he said. "So many, I think they starting to cancel each other out. I had two no-license tickets—one in Missouri and one in Kansas. Then I got two letters in the mail—one stated that Missouri was handing the warrant over to Kansas, and the other stated that Kansas was handing the warrant over to Missouri. I'm confused! Are they canceled, or did they just trade?"

I started laughing really hard. Completely out of my element. Then he started telling me about his homeboy that would catch the bus over his house and then ask for a ride home. A tight pain gripped my gut from laughing so hard.

"One time I tried to outsmart him," Marley continued. "I left the house early on his ass. But this Negro made the bus driver cut me off!"

"Marley, please stop," I laughed. "I can't take—"

Suddenly, I was yanked off my stool by the arm.

"What the hell are you doing?" Gideon asked me menacingly.

The sudden movement made me a little dizzy. And then I realized that, in the seven months I'd known Gideon, he'd never put his hands on me like that.

"Gideon, are you crazy?" I snapped at him.

"No, are *you* crazy? Rodrick is right upstairs. If he sees you talking to one of these niggas in his business partner's club, somebody will get fucked up."

"Oh, so it's okay for him to do whatever he wants to do?"

Marley stood up. "You okay, Tyesha?"

"She's fine," Gideon told him.

"I'm fine," I said.

Marley sat back down but kept an eye on me.

"Where's Kylie?" Gideon asked me.

"With my momma. I'm here to settle this shit between me and Rodrick," I said loudly over the music. "I'm tired of his bullshit."

"No, you not. You never will be. Go on home before you get in trouble."

"I thought you were on my side, Gideon."

"I'm on *my* side. I'm worried about *me*. If Rodrick comes down here and fucks shit up, I'ma be forced to fuck shit up wit' him. Because I can't let nothing happen to him. We sell dope together. He's my investment."

I was surprised by what I said next: "So now you mad because I wouldn't kiss you! You don't like me no more, huh?"

"It's not because you wouldn't kiss me. I don't like you because you weak. You let Rodrick walk all over you because yall got a child together. I don't like weak bitches."

"I'm weak now?"

"Stupid weak," he said firmly. "And gettin' weaker."

"I'ma show you weak. Where's Rodrick?"

"He's upstairs right now. He'll be down—"

I stormed off, jostling through the thick crowd. Holding the rail, I climbed the metal steps up to the next floor. There was a big, bearded man in an argyle sweater standing outside the door I needed to get in.

He started to hold his hand up. Then he squinted at me.

"Tyesha?"

"Yes, is Rodrick in there?"

I had no idea who this big man was. They rotated security all the time. I figured he knew me the same way everybody else I didn't know knew me—through Rodrick or The Site. Or both.

"I know you're Rodrick's BM," he said, "but I can't let you in right now."

"Why not?"

"They're handling business, you feel me?"

"I bet they are. That's why he just called me and told me to come down," I lied.

"He did?"

"Yes, I have his phone with his contacts."

"Aw, yeah, he was trippin' earlier about losing it. My fault, cutie." He turned the knob and held the door open for me. "Straight down the hall, make your first right."

The thick door shut on its own when I entered the hallway. As I walked down to the room, I heard one man's voice speaking in a monotonous tone. It was Rodrick's. I started speed walking.

"... and we thank You for getting these bricks here safely. We ask You, Lord, to bless all of us as we traffic this product that came from Your Earth. We ask for Your protection and Your strength to protect us from the captors ..."

I was awed that Rodrick had the whole room holding hands in prayer. They were standing around a huge table stocked with what looked like plastic-wrapped bricks of weird colored marijuana—light and dark green hairs, dirty oranges. And the room had a pungent smell that I could only compare to animal crackers. I had planned to rush in on him and beat his head in for even thinking about changing his relationship status without giving me a warning, but I could wait until he was finished with his prayer. I'd give him that courtesy.

"... and keep us from being bound. Because You teach us, Lord, that Your Word is not bound. We also ask You to protect our families as we go through our trials and tribulations. We ask You to touch Skooly's brother's heart and restore his consciousness as he recovers from his gunshot wound. We ask You to watch over our girlfriends and wives—and my soon-to-be wife and our 4-year-old daughter—as we risk our lives day in and day out to shelter them."

My bottom lip hung in shock. He referred to me as his soon-to-be-wife in front of all of his friends, and seemed so earnest about it. I wasn't on fire like I was when I walked up the steps, but I was still sizzling.

"We know, oh Lord, that we sin and walk in ways that aren't Your way," Rodrick continued, "but we ask you to show us Your way and guide us out of this game one day. We have so much to be thankful for and we praise You and ..."

One of the phones in my pocket beeped. And one of the men at the side of the table nearest me turned his head and I was noticed for the first time. He looked at me curiously—part what-are-you-doing-in-here, and part damn-you-look-good. I mouthed the word "sorry" and left the room.

With my back against the hallway wall, still listening to Rodrick finish up his prayer, I found which phone went off.

It was his.

And he had a notification.

I pressed the icon that took me to his messages. There was one from none other than the infamous Angela youngandfly Serrano. My anger tightened again as I read what she posted in his private inbox:

Angela youngandfly Serrano: hey handsome I'm outside the club right now standing in this long-ass line. can u come get me in or do I have to pay? U better get me in VIP in the next 2 minutes or I'ma leave with this brotha standing in front of me who smells like some of ur good-ass weed #ticktock

The ho was outside! I whisked down the hall and struggled out the thick door. I paced down the metal steps—I think Gideon saw me coming down. So I hurriedly pushed my way through the crowd. I got out the front door and saw the line of people stretching as far back as I could see.

"Is it packed in there?" a guy near the front of the line asked.

I ignored him and started walking quickly down the line, scanning the faces of the girls, giving them each a one-second glance.

Where the fuck are you, bitch?

Walking faster down the line, I saw a few light-skinned girls that could have resembled Angela youngandfly Serrano in the face, but none had the body to match. Angela's breasts were *huge,* according to the images in her photo album. And her butt was just as big.

119

Then I saw someone step out of line in a hurry, about thirty feet ahead of me. It was a girl that gave me a fleeting look of shock, wearing a dress far too small for her thickness. When the girl speed-walked down the sidewalk, her tush wobbled within her tight skirt, struggling to stay tucked in.

I was almost sure it was Angela!

"Hey!" I called.

The light-skinned girl looked back for a second, turned and started working her long legs harder. She was nearly running now.

"Angela!" I screamed, picking up the pace in my step. "I know that's you! Stop!"

But the girl didn't. In her high heels, she was moving unbelievably fast. It was clear she was trying to get away.

I pushed on, breaking into a full run. "C'mere, ho! Don't make me chase you!"

The girl ahead of me suddenly stopped from exhaustion. She turned around, planting her hands on her hips, fatigued. I halted when I saw the girl's face up close. I gasped.

"Deja?" I uttered her name in confusion.

She looked at me as if she were tired—not just from running, but from hiding the truth.

"Go ahead and cry," she said flatly.

As much as I didn't want to, I couldn't help it. The tears began to trickle, burning my cheeks.

"How long?" I asked her.

Sighing, she said, "We've been fuckin' since the day after he got out of prison. Of course, he was with you the first day. But we've been writing each other before he got out."

"Fa-real, Deja? Are you serious? Yall been makin' me look like a complete fool. I can't believe you! You put up this fake name on The Site, fake pictures, and that bitch has been you the whole time? I used to complain about her to you and you fuckin' played along. What did I do to you?"

"He was mine from the beginning," she retorted. "I told you I liked Rodrick back in high school. And not only did you steal him, you got pregnant by him too."

I wiggled my hands in my tight pockets nonchalantly.

My left hand found the brass knuckles my mother used to fight with in her gang days. My fingers prodded through the finger holes.

"You always thought you were better than me," she went on. "You teased me about being fat even when I decided to start working out with you. I was always the fat friend. You're little sidekick that had to sit back and watch all the niggas in school gawk over you."

I eased my fingers back out the holes. "Deja, I wasn't teasing you to be mean. I was trying to motivate you to lose weight. You always complained about being big and I wanted to help you. Look at you now. I helped you get there."

"No, *I* did this!" she screamed at me, flowing her hands over her curvaceous frame. "Don't try to take credit for this. That's all you do is take. You took my self-esteem. You took my dignity. And you took my man!"

"Them bitches is fightin'!" someone yelled from behind.

I turned for a second, then—

Bam!

Deja punched me so hard I don't know which side of my face she hit, as I found myself fighting with gravity. The wall of the building saved me from going down. Right when my eyes started working again, I saw Deja—clenching her teeth in rage—charging towards me. I covered my head as she swung at me again and carelessly struck the brick wall behind me. She howled in pain, and I seized the opportunity to grab her throat.

"Bitch!" I snarled.

She grabbed my throat too. We were choking each other.

Biting my lip in anger, I pushed her up against a parked car and made her do a back bend, slamming her head down against the hood. I squeezed harder and she started wheezing. Impulsively, she grabbed my wrists and tried to pry them off. She couldn't.

I wanted to kill her. "I'm tired of people fuckin' me!" I screamed. "No more! And it starts wit' you!"

There was a crowd around us now. I could hear the taunts and the laughter. Someone yelled out, "Don't break it up! I'm getting this shit on video!"

I grabbed her hair and slung her to the concrete. Deja looked furious. She kicked her heels at me but I got ahold of her ankles and threw them to the side. I dropped down on top of her and rained punches down on her savagely, with my bare fists.

The bridge of her nose split first.

Then her left eye turned bloodshot.

"Don't break it up! Get back yall! Let 'em fight!"

Fedbound Marley and **107 others** commented on a video **Tyesha816** was tagged
in.

August 17th, 2:00 p.m.

CHAPTER 10

Deja Michelle tilted her head back and let the second eye drop drip into her left eye. She blinked repeatedly as she dabbed the excess moisture with a tissue. Staring at her stark naked reflection in the mirror, she could barely recognize her face.

Her left jaw was swollen red. There was a half-inch gash on the bridge of her nose that was now sealed with a butterfly closure. On her neck, where Tyesha had stomped her, there was a nasty brown bruise. And her lip was busted.

She pulled her hair back and saw another bruise behind her ear. Titling her shoulder toward the mirror, she saw red scrapes on her back from the concrete. It looked like a tiger clawed her.

"I should press charges," she said.

"Deja, don't talk like that," Rodrick said. "Yall fought. It's over. Don't bring in the law."

She turned around immediately. Rodrick was sitting on the ruffled bed Indian-style, trying to figure out the operating system on his new phone. He didn't have on any clothes either.

She quickly snatched the phone from him and tried to log into The Site.

He shot to his feet. "What the fuck are you doing?!" he said, as he wrestled the phone back out of her hand.

"I was changing your status!"

"You not about to change shit," he retorted.

"Why not? You said you was, nigga! Are you gonna continue to make her think yall still together? Or am I the one getting played here?!"

He plopped back down on the bed and lowered his face into his palms, sighing.

"You need to make up your mind," Deja said. "Is it gonna be me or her?"

He kept his face buried, didn't say a word. She crossed her arms and waited. Since Junior High she had wanted Rodrick Brown to be her man. But he had never dated big girls back then. She waited until he got locked up, after he'd already had a child by Tyesha, to confess in a letter that she'd had a crush on him. To her surprise, he wrote back and said he'd liked her too. But not sexually, because he couldn't see himself sleeping with her because she thought lowly of herself. He told her if she didn't like herself, why should he? The very next day after she got his letter she started exercising with Tyesha. She saw improvements within a few months' time, and when she sent Rodrick pictures, he gave her glowing compliments and motivation. He taught her that God's Spirit dwelled within and that she simply had to let His spirit shine outward. What once was a crush became an intense desire to have his love. She sent him money weekly and went to see him every day Tyesha or his family wasn't there.

Deja's tear ducts began to well up.

"Me or her?" she asked again.

"Hold on," he said. "I'm waiting on God to give me an answer."

She thumped in the head. "I'm tired of waiting, Rodrick! I need you!"

"I can't think. Now is not the right time for this shit. Why did you make that post on my wall? You fucked everything up."

"That was my intentions. It forced you to make a decision." She touched the sides of his face and forced a kiss. She laid him out on the bed and straddled him. Her huge booty enveloped his whole waist. "And I need you to make the *right* decision, baby. Please?"

She arched her back and lifted her tush slightly. She reached around and grabbed ahold of his beefy member, but it was flaccid. She flopped it around in her fist, trying to agitate it.

"You can't get hard again?" she asked. "Is it my face?"

"No," he said. "It's Tyesha's face. I keep seeing it when I close my eyes. It's my daughter's face. I don't even have to close my eyes to see her. I can't do this no more, Deja. I have to go."

He shoved her to the side and started putting his clothes on.

Deja grabbed his arm desperately and hugged it to her busty chest. "Don't do this, Rodrick! Please, baby! Don't leave me!"

He pulled his arm free to slip into his LV zip hoodie. He walked out the room, and Deja would have chased him but the thought of him leaving made her nauseous and she made a dash for the toilet. She dropped to her knees and vomited into the bowl, crying hysterically as she heard her front door slam shut.

***

"Momma, it itches," Kylie whined.

I was driving on the highway and couldn't do much to help my daughter right now. "We're almost home. Stop scratching it, okay?"

"But it itches."

"Rub it. Don't scratch."

There was no way in hell I was going to let my daughter spend the night at her grandmother's house again. Kylie had an inch-long razor cut on her forearm from digging in one of my mother's boxes. As she pulled out, a blade sliced her open. Velma Fenty said it wasn't that bad of a cut, but any cut on my daughter was bad. And how old was the blade? My daughter could be infected.

First thing tomorrow morning I was going to put her back in daycare. I took her out of the last one because the ghetto staff there didn't feed her adequately. She was always hungry when I went to pick her up. I hated that I might possibly have to choose between hunger and harm, but I'd choose a little hunger any day. Hopefully this new daycare off 350 Highway that one of my Site friends recommended would be a great facility.

"I saw Uncle *La'killer* today," my daughter said.

My brow creased in confusion. "You saw who?"

"Uncle *La'killer*."

I prayed I was hearing her wrong. "Did you say Lady-killer?"

She nodded.

"Where did you see him?" I asked, my heart rate escalating.

"Today. At mall."

"Where was your grandmother at?"

"In the *bafroom*. I wait on da bench and he see me."

"Did you tell your grandmother?"

"No. He told me not tell her."

"Kylie, you listen to me. If you ever see that man again, you scream, okay? He's not your uncle."

"Okay, Momma."

When we got home, I tore off her Band-Aid and checked out the cut. It was sealed, thankfully. I put some peroxide and Neosporin on it, stuck another Band-Aid on her and told her to go lay down. I needed to lay down myself. My head still felt fuzzy from the alcohol I downed last night and I couldn't sleep because I had been crying into my pillow until six this morning. The knuckles on my left pinky and ring finger were swollen painfully but I still found myself sitting at my desktop computer, typing in my password.

In a couple clicks, The Site was on my screen.

I was shocked to see I had more notifications than I ever had in my life. On my wall was a video that I was tagged in, which was linked to a popular hiphop website. The thumbnail was a blur of two women fighting, and it instantly registered that me and Deja's brawl had been caught on tape. My heart started beating faster as I clicked the play button and the video started streaming.

The first frame was of me choking Deja up against the hood of a black Chrysler 300. The camera was extremely shaky, from some boy filming us on his smartphone. A second later, I threw Deja to the ground, and that's when her breasts flopped out.

"Oh my God," I gasped.

The camera boy zoomed in on her nipples. *"Don't break it up!"* he yelled in amusement. *"Get back yall! Let 'em fight!"*

I watched myself pummel her face in and I couldn't believe it was me. The camera circled around and got another close up—between Deja's legs.

As I looked at the footage, I started to get teary-eyed. I didn't mean for Deja to get embarrassed like this in front of the world. I just wanted to beat her ass. Shaking my head, I tapped the Esc button and clicked on the comments.

Harold the Moneyman: She got knocked the fuck out!

Shake-it Girl12: This remind me of one of Floyd Mayweather's fights.

Julius Taylor: Damn, I didn't know Tyesha had hands like that.

Velma Fenty: That's my baby! I didn't raise no punks!

Rita RealSpit Gibson: Can yall stop commenting on this, please? These are human beings yall are making fun of. Two beautiful women who were friends with each other. Let's try to bring them up, not celebrate their disagreement.

Michael StreetLawyer: I don't know if this is an assault case or manslaughter.

VVS Vernon: I don't care what yall say. That girl getting her ass beat is fine. You see them nipples? You see that pussy? I'd still take her out to eat, even if I gotta feed her through a straw.

Fedbound Marley: @Tyesha816. Oh, so that's what you meant! LOL! If you need bond money, I got you, player. I sold out last night!

A wistful smile appeared on my face. Marley was just joking but I was worried that I could really face charges. And I wished my mother wouldn't have commented, but what could I do about it? My emotions were doing somersaults right now.

My phone started ringing. I looked down at the screen and saw Rodrick's face. I tapped the volume once and his call silenced.

I leaned back in my chair and started to question my love for him. He'd put me through so much bullcrap. But if I pushed him out of my life, how would Kylie take it?

Would she blame me when she got older? I didn't know what to do. Times like this I would call Deja and we'd talk for hours. I felt like I had nobody now.

Well, I had one person. I had my Kylie. I got up and was on my way to lay down with her when there was a knock at my door.

I looked through my peep hole and, closing my eyes as a tear fell, I sighed heavily.

"Tyesha!" Rodrick called out, knocking again. "I know you in there. Let me in, baby!"

"Go away!" I screamed.

"I'm sorry. I know that don't mean much right now but I'm saying it anyway. I'm stupid as fuck, I know. You probably think I'm the most trifling nigga in the world."

"Probably?! Get the fuck away from my house! You hurt me *sooo* bad, Rodrick. My whole adult life has been dedicated to you, and you repay me by pissing on me *constantly*. I can't think of what I've done to deserve this."

He jiggled the knob in vain. "You didn't do anything, Tyesha, baby. It was me. I made so many mistakes, trying to please everybody. But I realized it doesn't work like that. I'm supposed to be with you and you only. God gave me an answer."

"He gave me one too!" I shouted through the door. "He told me to tell you to get the hell away from my house! I'm through, Rodrick! I'm done!"

"Just open the door so we can talk. Please?"

"No!"

He kicked the door. I looked through the peep hole and saw him with his hands on his hips in frustration. I didn't care what he said—he wasn't getting in this house.

"When can I see my daughter again?" he asked calmly.

"We'll work something out," I said.

"Okay."

He trotted back down my steps and disappeared into the day. Honestly, if it weren't for Kylie, I wouldn't care if I ever saw him again.

Rodrick Al-Bashir: "For if ye forgive men their trespasses, your heavenly Father will also forgive you. But if ye forgive not men their trespasses, neither will your Father forgive your trespasses." Matthew 6:14-15

August 18th, 6:44 a.m.

CHAPTER 11

Moonlight still bullied the dark sky as I walked out of my house the next morning. As I neared my G6 in my driveway, getting my ignition key ready, I saw a white four-door BMW parked on my side of the street.

What the fuck?!

It was dark out, but the man in the Beamer looked like Ladykiller. So when the car cut on its headlights and pulled forward, I got in my car and sped to catch up, barreling down E. 67th Street and across James A. Reed Road. I was going to pull alongside the car at the stop sign at the end of the street to be sure it wasn't him, but as we neared the corner, the BMW zoomed through the sign without slowing down.

I stopped and watched the white car propel off into the distance, the tail lights growing ever smaller. My heart rate began to slow down.

Maybe it wasn't him. Maybe I'm seeing things.

***

As soon as twelve o' clock hit, I went to the break room and pulled me out a seat. For lunch, I packed myself a grilled chicken sandwich with ranch dressing leftover from last night. I sipped some of my low-sodium tomato juice—it's supposed to protect from numerous cancers—and flicked the lock off my phone's display.

I didn't know what to update my status with. What was I supposed to post after being captured on video beating my best friend's ass? I wasn't going to gloat; that wasn't classy. I wasn't going to apologize either; Deja would have to do that first. And even if she did, I didn't think I would give her one in return.

The video had reached over 400 Likes. What worried me the most was not knowing if my supervisor would see it and try to terminate me. As far as I knew, Ruth didn't have a Site page, but one never knew these days. If my mother had one, Ruth could have one. To be on the safe side, I tapped the video link and deleted it from my page.

Then I went to Rodrick's and read his status.

I couldn't help but think it was directed toward me. It was sad. He was trying to force me to forgive him by using a scripture. A trademark Rodrick Brown move: make somebody else feel guilty to get his way. I wanted to comment on his status and ask him how many times was a person supposed to forgive a habitual liar and cheater, but I knew he'd respond with something slick and we'd go back and forth over the internet and both end up looking like idiots. I thought about changing my relationship status—he'd get the picture then. But I knew if I changed it, guys would be messaging me like crazy and I didn't want any new attention right now.

And, I hated to admit ... deep down ... I wanted to see if Rodrick would get a wake-up call this time and see that I was the woman he needed. I know I'd said I didn't care if I ever saw him again ... well, it still held true if he didn't change.

"You always on yo phone."

I looked up and saw Stuart Bradshaw sitting across from me. He was the security guard over the DMV. Eagerly, he started taking the clear wrap off his bowl of turkey salad.

"So?" I said jokingly.

"You know I got handcuffs, right?"

"And I got pepper spray."

"Do you?"

"No."

He laughed. And after gobbling down a few forkfuls of salad, he said, "Ruth told me to keep an eye on you. She told me to tell her if I saw you on your phone while on the clock."

"I hate that B."

"Me too. I wonder if she got somebody watching me to see when I get on *my* phone."

I chuckled. Stuart was my Site friend also, though he rarely made updates. His girlfriend, Joanne Dunley, however, posted every five minutes, it seemed. And they were some of the bitterest stats ever. It seemed like every other day she had an issue in her life—car broke down, dog died, airborne virus, stress bumps. I was surprised Stuart was still with her.

"How's Joanne?" I asked.

Shaking his head, he replied, "I don't know. She's at home right now looking for a job. She got fired for writing up the owner. I told her not to do that."

"That sucks."

"Yeah, it does. And I'm sorry I couldn't make it to yo daughter's birthday party. I had to go get her car fixed and when I went to pay for it, her card got denied and I didn't have mine on me—"

"You don't have to explain. I understand what you're dealing with."

"Thank you," he said.

He finished his meal and got up to leave. Before he walked out the break room, he turned back toward me with a knowing grin.

"I'll see you later, Mayweather."

149

I blushed. But how could I be surprised that he'd seen the video?

My phone beeped in my hand. I had a notification. When I clicked on it, I saw that Rodrick had tagged me in his status update about forgiveness. Now the stat showed up on my profile page. He was trying to make sure I saw it, and I know he wanted me to respond.

I wasn't going to give him the pleasure.

***

When I walked in the new daycare center, I had no idea where the kids were. I had no idea where anybody was. The place was empty.

"Hello?" I said softly.

I pushed through the first set of doors I saw and was surprised to see at least thirty kids sitting on the floor, legs crossed, paying close attention to the police officer at the front. I thought this was some kind of drill until one of the staff members came up to me.

Her eyes were full of grief. "Which child is yours?"

STATUS

My eyes scanned the rows of kids. I didn't see Kylie.

"I don't see her," I said.

The woman swallowed. "Was her name Kylie Brown?"

Was? I repeated to myself, looking confused. *Why was she speaking about my daughter in the past tense?*

"Her name *is* Kylie Brown?" I corrected her. "What's going on?"

"Your child is missing."

CHAPTER 12

I called Rodrick to find out if he picked Kylie up. When he told me he didn't even know where the daycare was, the reality of my daughter being kidnapped became very real. My chest felt tight, skin started to perspire, and I felt dizzy all of a sudden.

I had to sit down. But as soon as the police officer pulled out a chair for me, I shot back to my feet. "Find my daughter now!"

"That's what we're trying to do," said the officer, placing his hand on my shoulder. "Calm down. Is there anybody else who could've picked her up?"

My mind raced. And then a surge of hope went through me. Why didn't I think of her sooner? I called my mother fast and asked her did she have Kylie.

"No," my mother said, and my heart sank. "Am I supposed to?"

"These people at this daycare can't find her. Momma, I'ma loose it here in about ten seconds!"

"Have you called Rodrick yet?" she asked with panic in her voice.

"I just talked to him. He didn't even know where the fuckin' daycare was. Momma, what am I supposed to do?!"

"She's probably just hiding somewhere. You know she likes to hide. It's her first day at that daycare. Maybe she went off by herself and got lost."

I watched a parent walk past with two of her kids, straight out the door. The rest of the kids were still sitting on the floor. They looked restless, probably would rather be playing. Tears started to come down my cheeks.

"Momma, I'ma call you back."

"I'm on my way. Keep it together, Tyesha."

I put the phone in my pocket and threw my hands up helplessly. "I don't know where she is. I need to find her. *I need my daughter!*"

I collapsed into the seat and started sobbing into my hands.

The cop said, "Are you sure no one else could have picked her up?"

"No!" I shouted. "What kind of place would let anybody come get her? There are only three people that are allowed to pick her up—myself, Velma Fenty, and Rodrick Brown. None of them have her!"

The same daycare staff member that told me my child was missing came over after the cop called her. He asked her a couple questions about the safety precautions they used to make sure kids didn't fall into the wrong hands. According to policy, anybody coming to pick up a child had to sign off. Nobody signed for Kylie.

Then the lady told us some news that stirred me to the core.

"One of the children mentioned that they saw Kylie leave out the back with a man. I'm not sure how accurate a 5-year-old can be, but I don't want to leave it out if it helps."

I instantly responded, "What did the man look like?"

"He said the man had a light skin color and was tall. But to a 5-year-old, everybody's tall, right?"

The cop started to open his mouth to ask her a question but I cut him off. "Where is the boy?" I asked hurriedly.

She led us to the back of the seated children and pointed to a Black boy with a stylish design in his head, fingering for him to come over. He got up and walked over in a casual pace. He blinked at us all, just an innocent child. But to me he could possibly be my daughter's savior.

"What complexion was he, baby?" I questioned. "Was he light like this woman here?" I asked, touching the staff member's arm next to me, a white woman with a pasty skin tone. "Or was his complexion more like mine?"

The boy scrunched his face, thinking hard as his eyes jumped between us both.

Me and the staff member's skin color were close. I hadn't had much sun lately, other than the pool party, so my hue was on the lighter side. But clearly our tones were different. I still had color, more of a warm yellow. The staff member had almost no color, nearly pure white. And up her forearms her skin was dotted with tiny sun spots, which made her skin look even whiter.

The boy pointed to me.

"Okay, I have another question," I said. "What did his hair look like? Was it black and cut low?"

"I don't know. He had on a hat," the boy said.

I breathed out my nose. "You said he was tall. Was he my height, or a lot taller like this officer here."

The cop straightened up to his full height of 5'11". I was four inches shorter than him.

The boy's eyebrows dipped in concentration, then he turned and said, "That tall," pointing to Gideon, who had just walked in the room with Rodrick.

Gideon was maybe 6'3".

Around the same height as Ladykiller.

I squatted down and grabbed the boy by his arms, looking deeply into his eyes. I had one more question that would tell me if Ladykiller took my child.

"When you saw the man and my daughter leaving out the back door, was he carrying her? Did she scream?"

"No," the boy replied, shaking his head. "She was smiling. She was holding the man's hand."

Tyesha816 shared a photo

Tyesha816: My daughter is missing and the police won't report it until 24 hours!!!! Fuck the KCPD!! Please, if you see this little girl, inbox me!!! Please!!!

August 18th, 9:06 p.m.

CHAPTER 13

"I didn't say we wouldn't look for your daughter," said Detective Rosan, as we stood outside the daycare center near his black Dodge Charger, the red strobe on his dash spinning round and round. He had a kind, honest face and clean white teeth—though one at the bottom was chipped. The black leather bomber jacket he wore gave me the impression that he was about business. "I just said we won't report it until another 24 hours. We don't want to get everybody worked up for nothing. She might be at a family member's house, or a friend's house. We can't rule that out yet."

"The hell we can't!" I yelled. "I called everybody before you got here. Nobody I know has her. I'm trying to tell you who took my daughter. It was Ladykiller! Go arrest him!"

Rodrick was standing behind me squeezing my upper arms gently. Then his thumbs went to the middle of my back and massaged my spine. Though there was no easing the tension in my body, it did feel good. Gideon was perched on the daycare's wall not too far from where we stood. He was in earshot for sure. And he was staring at me with intense, grievous eyes. I couldn't help but wonder if he felt he should be standing here with me and not Rodrick.

"We have somebody checking into the Ladykiller story," said the detective, patting the air with his hand as if to tell me to lower my voice. "I'm trying to help you. I have a daughter too and I don't know what I'd do if she came up missing."

"I don't wanna hear that. I wanna hear that you found my daughter! And standing around here asking me questions isn't making that happen!"

Rodrick's thumbs pressed harder.

"Can I talk to you two privately for a minute?" Rosan asked.

I was fuming, but me and Rodrick walked over to the side of the building with him, the only area that wasn't crowded with police officers and nosy news people standing around.

He put a hand on each of our shoulders and dipped his head to look into our eyes. "I'm going to find your daughter, okay? There are certain procedures that we have to go through first. But I'm going to overlook all of them and get this search started. Tell me more about this Ladykiller person you're talking about."

I started by telling him about how often Ladykiller commented on my status updates. The detective's face showed doubt, so I made it a point to tell him that Ladykiller's presence on my page was abnormal. It wasn't until I explained to him how crazy Ladykiller was—the "chance" meeting at the gym *and* at my job, the possible sighting at my house, my daughter pronouncing Ladykiller's name when she said she saw him at the mall—that the detective's eyes started to glow with belief and shock.

My phone chimed once in my pocket and I pulled it out. I had just received a text from Gideon.

Gideon: Come back to the front real quick

Excusing myself, I raced over to where Gideon was sitting. He pointed at the screen of his phone, then gave it to me for me to read.

"I knew he posted on yo page a lot," Gideon said, "but I didn't know it was that serious."

"This is The Site," I said with surprise. "I thought you didn't have a page."

"I don't. But when you said you thought Ladykiller took Kylie, I logged in to see who he was. Look what he posted."

It was the comments feed from my status update about the KCPD not helping me find Kylie. I started reading.

God's Angel: I'm praying for you and your daughter!

Trillyoung Sav: If yo daughter was white, they would've found her by now

STATUS

Fedbound Marley: You and your daughter are in my prayers too

Atlanta Baby: I can't believe anybody would take that precious little girl!

Velma Fenty: My granddaughter is coming home. We'll go out and search ourselves, fuck them.

Bobby Mason: Me and my frat brothers will help you with the search party

Deja: i know you still might be mad at me but kylie is still my goddaughter and i'm praying for you and her text me if you need anything

Holly Carter: God will bring your daughter home. Trust and believe. I'm praying hard.

Quita Wheeler: OMG! @Tyesha816 I'm crying for you. This is horrible!

CousinPete: Did this little girl really get taken? Or is this SPAM?

VVS Vernon: I hate seeing shit like this. Whoever took her needs to be shot in the streets like the old days.

Rita RealSpit Gibson: I just inboxed you a number to a private detective if the KCPD won't help. I'm praying for you as well.

Joanne Dunley: All my love and prayers are going out to you and Kylie tonight

I kept reading, looking for whatever it was that Gideon wanted me to see. But all I was seeing was a whole bunch of posts from people wishing me and Kylie well. The posts, though, seemed to revitalize my energy. I felt a stronger sense of hope knowing I had so many people—some of which I never met—in my corner.

Finally, I asked Gideon what he was talking about. He took the phone back and scrolled back up to where I started. There was a comment I didn't see, right above God's Angel's post, and he showed it to me.

Ladykiller: You'll find her soon

It floored me. I read the four words over and over, trying to interpret the meaning. Was he saying he was going to give her back? Would she still be alive?

I told Gideon I was going to show the comment to the detective.

"Okay," he said. "But bring my phone back when you're done. I have to make a run. Let Rodrick know too. If yall need anything, just call."

Quickly, I reached in and gave him a hug. "Be safe," I said.

"I will, Tyesha."

I kissed him on the cheek.

Then I paced back over to the side of the building, where the detective was explaining to Rodrick what he could do through social media to help expedite the return of our daughter.

Rosan stopped mid-sentence when he saw the urgency in my eyes.

"What is it?" Rosan asked.

"Ladykiller just responded to my status update. Look at it."

He read the screen and said, "Can you respond back to him?"

"Yeah. What am I supposed to say?"

"Ask him what he wants. Then try to get him to meet you somewhere. Kidnappers usually want a ransom. But in your case, it seems like he's more infatuated with you as a woman than anything else. He's a stalker, so he might not want money. He might want to trade you for her. Let's find out."

I used my own phone to go to Ladykiller's page. I clicked on the message icon so anything I posted would be private between me and him. My first post was a question asking him what he wanted from me. It took him exactly six minutes to respond.

Tyesha816: What do you want from me?

Ladykiller: I want you to have your daughter back.

Tyesha816: How do I get her back?

Ladykiller: Keep looking. Don't give up.

Tyesha816: Look where?!

Ladykiller: I don't know. But I'll help you.

I turned to the detective. I was frustrated with the conversation already. "He's playing games with me," I cried. "He's not gonna give her back!"

"Yes, he will," the detective assured me. "If he wants you to play a game, then we have to play. The ball is in his court right now. It looks like he's gonna give you clues. Ask him can you meet him somewhere for the first clue. If he's as obsessed with you as it seems, he won't turn down a chance to see you again face to face."

Looking down at my phone, I started tapping letters with my thumb.

Tyesha816: Okay, I need your help.

Ladykiller: Let me know what you need me to do.

Tyesha816: Can you meet me somewhere?

Ladykiller: Name the place.

CHAPTER 14

I sat on a bench at the Crown Center Square Fountain on Grand Boulevard, a line of shade trees behind me nearly hiding me in darkness. I stared at the water spouting out of the fountains in front of me and felt angry tears welling up in my eyes. This is where I took Kylie on her third birthday. She had played in this very Square with one of her cousins of the same age, screaming with sheer joy whenever she got splashed.

Kylie always loved the water.

I tried my hardest to blink back the tears and stay focused.

The boulevard was deserted. Just me ... sort of. There was a staircase to my right leading up to a row of manicured bushes, where Detective Rosan promised me there'd be two cops hiding in wait. Maybe fifty yards in front of me, on top of the Halls building, there was a railing protecting the roof's edge where a sniper was supposed to be positioned, but I didn't see him. I hoped he was there. And if he was, would he be able to get a good shot through the trees?

I turned quickly when I caught sight of a man walking casually down the sidewalk. Tonight's half moonlight wasn't enough to get a good look at him, but I could see he had on a backpack.

I was startled by my own phone when it buzzed in my hand. I had a text message.

Detective Rosan: Is it him?

I couldn't tell yet. But as the unknown man drew near, I suddenly realized that he was closer to me than any of the officers in hiding. This man could beat me to a pulp before they cleared the stairs.

The sniper, I reminded myself, taking deep breaths. *The sniper will get him.*

STATUS

My thumb instinctively hovered over the "y" on my phone's keypad. But when the man with the backpack got close enough for me to see his face, my thumb went down to the "n" and I typed in "no." The man was old with a dirty white beard. Probably just a homeless wanderer.

A Metro bus thundered down the boulevard then, its headlights and MAX route display waking up the darkness. I had forgotten how loud and scary buses were at night time. It stopped across the street from me, and a couple seconds later it was drudging off again.

And suddenly there was a man standing on the bus stop. No, not standing anymore but *running* across the street towards me!

I typed in "yes" and hit send as quick as I could. This was Ladykiller racing up to me, tall and slender. I could see the whites of his eyes now as he cleared the curb.

The plan was to sit and talk with Ladykiller for a moment to make sure he was really who he was. Detective Rosan hoped I could even get him to admit that he kidnapped my daughter, and then they would come storming out of hiding with their machine guns out.

Fuck that!

I got up and started running in the opposite direction. I was scared out of my mind.

"Tyesha!" Ladykiller called after me.

I pumped my legs so fast I almost lost my balance. Stupidly, I looked back, my long hair flipping over my shoulder—and I saw Ladykiller gaining on me.

"Tyesha, stop! Come back!"

That's when I heard the first shot. Ladykiller shooting at me or the sniper shooting at him, I didn't know. But I was still on my feet. Then I did another stupid thing—I looked back again, I couldn't help it. Ladykiller was still on his feet too, and a lot closer than before.

As I climbed the stairway, panting as hard as I ever had before in my life, I saw the two officers hustling down with their guns in their hands. I passed them and ran behind the bushes, hunkering down out of sight and not caring about the stench of those officers' cigarette butts.

"Freeze! Get on the ground!"

I didn't look. I stayed crouched.

"I said freeze!"

"I didn't do anything," I heard Ladykiller say. "What did I do?"

"Hands in the air or we'll shoot!"

Seconds went by without a word. And then I heard the sound of a short scuffle and what I hoped was Ladykiller being taken to the ground.

"You have the right to remain silent. Anything you say *can and will* be used against you in the court of law."

"I can't get arrested," Ladykiller wailed in a way that made me think he was suddenly sorry for what he did. "I can't go to jail, *please*. Tyesha, help me! TYESHA!"

I closed my eyes and covered my ears.

Tyesha816: Kidnapper in custody! I'm closer to finding my daughter!

August 19th, 1:13 a.m.

CHAPTER 15

Questions ran through my mind as I sat inside the interrogation room with my arms crossed on the table, my head down, staring at the gray wall. I was in deep thought, waiting on a detective to come in and tell me they found my daughter.

Why did he take her? How could any man be that obsessed with me? Would they lock him up for life or would they give him a light sentence? Will I have to deal with this again?

I started looking at Ladykiller's profile page on my phone, trying to find answers. Most of the activity on his page pertained to messages to me or comments on my status updates. It was as if his whole page was created solely to interact with me. I scrolled further back through his timeline, as far back as a year, and I saw a post that I had never seen before. It was a message my mother, Velma Fenty, posted on Ladykiller's wall. It read: "I said no! I want nothing to do with you or your family! Stay out of my inbox!"

That was strange.

Suddenly, I heard a commotion outside of the room. I got up and went to the door and tried to open it, but it was locked. They locked me in!

"What's the problem?!" I heard Rodrick yell on the other side of the door.

Oh my God! I thought. Rodrick and my mother were waiting in the lobby for them to release me—as if I was guilty of something. *I should have told him not to come!*

"I don't wanna hear it!" an officer yelled. "Hands behind your back!"

Rodrick's voice came back hard. "I'm here trying to find my daughter and yall gone arrest me?! What part of the game is this?!"

"There's a pick-up warrant against you, Mr. Brown."

"So what?"

"So you have to"—I heard a chair being pushed back, maybe the officers hemming him up—"Don't fight us. Then you'll get resisting arrest, buddy."

I went back to my chair and plopped down in it. I grabbed my forehead and started crying. My family was disappearing!

When the door opened, I looked up. I recognized both of the detectives that walked in. Detective Frisk and Detective Copeland.

"Where's my baby's father?" I asked.

"He's in lockup now," said Frisk, taking a seat on the other side of the table.

Copeland leaned against the wall in another tight T-shirt, a blue one this time, and gave me a strict glare. "Thanks for bringing him to us," he said sarcastically.

"Fuck you!" I shouted. "Yall worried about arresting my baby daddy, but where's my DAUGHTER!"

"That's what we're in here to talk to you about." Frisk interlaced his fingers on the table. "When was the last time you saw her?"

"I'm not going through this shit again! I've answered

all of those questions a thousand times. Where's Detective Rosan?"

"He's off the case," Frisk said. "It was handed over to us."

"Did Ladykiller tell you where my daughter was?"

Frisk's lips where tight. Then he said, "Ladykiller was interrogated thoroughly. But he didn't tell us where your daughter was."

I felt the tears coming back. And I think I was having a sudden shortness of breath.

Detective Frisk told his partner to run and get me a cup full of water. He handed me a Styrofoam cup with a coffee lid on it. I opened it and drank slowly.

"It doesn't mean we're not going to find her," Frisk told me. "We just have to keep looking elsewhere."

"What do you mean 'elsewhere'?" I asked. "Ladykiller took my daughter. You have to push him till he cracks."

"Ms. Fenty, we're gonna end up releasing Ladykiller. He admitted that he had a heavy presence on your profile page, but he adamantly denied taking your daughter. We don't have enough evidence to hold him for very long."

"Why don't you put a tail on him and follow him to Kylie?" I asked desperately.

"We know where he lives. And we've talked to his mother, whom he stays with. Ms. Fenty, are you aware that Ladykiller is only seventeen years old?"

I gasped. "No ..."

"His real name is Landon Roby and his mother's name is Deborah Roby. From what his mother explained, all he does all day when he's not at school is type on his computer. And he's not at school much because he's one of those half-day seniors. According to a few of his teachers, he's actually a good student. His mother told us that if he had taken a 4-year-old child she would have known about it."

I was shaking my head. I couldn't understand it all. And why did Ladykiller's mother's name sound so familiar?

"I have to ask you some more questions," the detective said, his tone becoming harsh. "I've turned up a lot of interesting things during the course of this investigation. So I have to ask you, ma'am, how long have you had a violent streak?"

Blinking, I said, "What are you talking about?"

Copeland butted in. "You know what he's talking about."

"I've come across several things that have disturbed me and I have to follow up on them." Frisk reached into the inside pocket of his suit jacket and pulled out a folded sheet of paper. He unraveled it and looked it over. "I came across a popular hiphop website that featured a video of you going toe-to-toe with another female. Can you explain that to me?"

"It was just a fight that got caught on tape."

He nodded. "I went further back and found that you broke into a woman named ..." He squinted at the sheet. "... Dava Babcock's apartment. You proceeded to beat her and were subsequently arrested and put on a year's probation."

"Are you serious? In your little research you found, did you also see that my baby's daddy put a restraining order out on Dava? She was crazy. She was stalking the both of us and even threatened my daughter on The Site, which you should have record of. Hell yeah I went over there and kicked her ass. I'd do it again."

"Ms. Fenty, I also found that someone called the Department of Family Services on you for striking your daughter. The report read that you struck her several times for allegedly crying too loud."

"That's a fucking lie!" I shouted. "I know it was Dava Babcock who called DFS on me. She was just trying to get my daughter taken away from me because she was jealous of my relationship with Rodrick. What are you trying to say to me, detective?"

He stared me down. "Have you ever physically abused your daughter, Kylie Brown?"

I slapped him. I don't think I slapped him hard but I know I woke him up. His eyes were wide and he shot to his feet, only to stop Copeland from coming after me. He adjusted the collar of his suit jacket.

"Don't ever accuse me of hurting my own daughter," I cried, pointing my finger up at him. Tears streaked down my cheeks. "I would never lay a finger on my daughter. Never!"

Tyesha816: What did I do to deserve this?

August 19th, 11:25 a.m.

CHAPTER 16

"**Tyesha, put your** seatbelt on," my mother said to me again.

I ignored her. It was raining heavily outside and it seemed as if the windshield wipers could barely keep up. But what was the worst thing that could happen? We could skid off road and smack a guardrail, but we wouldn't roll over. My mother was driving too slow for that. And what if I did end up dying? Without Kylie, I already felt dead. A car crash might do me a favor.

Scrolling through the comments again, I hoped to stumble upon some sort of lead. But there was nothing but well wishes. And I was starting to see a few people had made assumptions that my daughter hadn't been kidnapped at all. I came across a comment from somebody suggesting that I might have abducted my own daughter and I felt anger singe into my veins. My thumb started typing a response on its own: *Fuck you!* But I didn't post it. I deleted it because there was no point in responding to people's cruel, attention-seeking remarks. The comment was linked to another social media network, one reported to be more popular than The Site. I followed the link and it took me to where the comment originated—I had a profile page on this site too but rarely used it—and saw that there were even more hateful comments from people under the trending topics #tyeshafenty and #tyesha816. Several local news stations had aired a brief segment on me and Kylie over the past few hours and it looked like people were drawing their own conclusions.

Samantha Hemp: She blamed her daughter's kidnapping on somebody from The Site. I don't believe it. #tyeshafenty

Gary Rezoni: The "stalker" she said took her daughter was a minor! #tyeshafenty #tyesha816 #crazybitch

STATUS

Swagirl42: Nine times out of ten it's the parents that did something to their own child. #numbersdontlie #tyeshafenty #guilty

RozayBlack: People don't kidnap Black kids. Ijs. #tyesha816 #tyeshafenty

Keoni Badd: Her daughter is way too beautiful. If she did it, I hope she gets life in prison. #tyeshafenty

Channel 12 News: "… daughter still missing. Detectives suspect mother of foul play …" #tyeshafenty #newstory #C12News

the prettiest troll: Did you see how big her daughter's forehead is? O_o #tyeshafenty #tyesha816

Stephen's Wife: I normally don't pass judgment before all the facts is out, but this just sounds fishy … #tyesha816 #tyeshafenty

I closed my phone and put it in my pocket. My mother asked me once more to put my seatbelt on so I just pulled it across my chest and clicked it in the socket out of re-spect for her.

When we got to her house and she was unlocking the front door in a hurry to get us out of the downpour, she noticed how red my eyes were from crying.

"Go upstairs and lay down," she said. "If you need me just holler."

My mother wouldn't let me go to my house alone, as bad as I wanted to. I really didn't want to step into her clutter. It was madness—madness I didn't need right now. But I couldn't say no. I was here.

I felt like a zombie as I plodded up her stairs, drag-ging my own feet. My clothes were wet from the rain but changing outfits was the last thing on my mind.

When I walked into the room that once belonged to me, the tears began again. This was the room I grew up in as a child. But now this was Kylie's room whenever she came over to grandma's. Almost all of her toys were pink, and on the walls were scribbled pictures of cartoon characters, trees, and even colorful stick figures she drew of us as a family—Rodrick was the tallest stick figure with black lines for dreads, I was next with scribbled black hair and a triangle skirt, and then Kylie drew herself with a smile bigger than the outline of her simple face.

By the bed, I dropped to my knees and put my elbows on the comforter, clasping my hands together in prayer. I pleaded with God to deliver me from this torture. I was babbling, snot running down my nose.

"I just want her back, Lord! Please, I can't take this!"

Feeling lightheaded, I laid down on the floor and stared at the ceiling. The bulbs around the ceiling fan were bright and blinding but all I could do was lay there and stare at the light, begging-wishing-pleading for this nightmare to be over. I started to hiccup as I cried, like I used to as a child. I couldn't remember the last time I balled my eyes out like this. I wondered if Kylie was crying right now. Was she okay? Was she hurt? Not knowing made my bones begin to tremble.

My body couldn't take anymore.

Then I rolled to my feet and looked inside the closet. There was a white jump rope with pink handles tangled around toys and stuffed animals. I untangled it and cut the ends off the jump rope with tiny pink scissors. I took a chair and pushed it dead center under the ceiling fan and, after unstrapping my gladiator sandals, I carefully stepped onto it barefoot, wobbling a little because the legs weren't even.

On my tiptoes, I reached high past the wooden blades. The chair shook unsteadily, as I tied one end of the jump rope around the rod pipe connected to the fan's motor. I pulled up the other end of the rope and tried to tie a noose.

But the rope kept coming undone.

"Dammit!" I fussed, sniffing the snot back in my nose. "How do you do this shit?"

I threw the rope down and let it hang, as I pulled my phone out of my pocket and did an internet search for "how to make a noose." I memorized the steps, pulled the rope back into my hands and began tying it deliberately.

After I was done, I compared it with the internet image. It looked the same.

So I placed it around my neck and drew it up tight and secure.

My face had never been this wet. The tears poured down my cheeks, dripping off my jaw onto my T-shirt.

Looking at my phone again, I loaded up The Site. I stared at my status update box, trying to think of some last dying words that I could share with the world. Maybe I could post a philosophical stat to let other women know how precious their children were. Or maybe I could find a quote that summed up my love for my daughter and how I couldn't live without her.

When I shifted my weight to my right foot, one of the chair's legs cracked in half. I lost my balance, accidentally kicked the chair out from under me and my neck suddenly tightened in excruciating pain.

I couldn't breathe!

I was suspended in the air by the jump rope, thrashing my arms and legs deliriously.

It was only causing me to swing, the rope to tighten. I struggled for air, dropped my phone and grabbed at the rope around my neck. I was clawing at my own throat. My fingernails drew blood.

"*Ughghgh,*" I choked.

195

My eyes felt like they were about to pop out the sockets. I tried to stretch my foot, an effort to hook my toes around the bed post, but it was out of reach. The ceiling fan repositioned and white dust sprinkled down on me. But it didn't break.

And the room began to darken.

Death began to close in on me.

I didn't want to do this anymore!

My mother must have heard the chair smack the floor because she came bursting into the room. She quickly hugged my legs and lifted up.

"Tyesha, take the rope off now!"

I fumbled with the rope and finally got it off, falling over on the bed because my mother couldn't hold my weight. I was coughing terribly. I wasn't out the water yet.

"*Breathe*, girl." She pushed my wild her away from my face. "*Breathe*."

Then my coughing started to get better.

"I'm sorry, Momma," I wheezed out.

"Baby, it's gonna get better," she said, hugging me to her chest. "We're gonna find Kylie."

"I'm so sorry …"

"None of this is your fault. You just had a moment of weakness. Everything's all right now. But from here on out, I need you to be strong. Kylie needs you to be strong."

"I will, Momma."

For the rest of the night my mother held me as I cried. And she cried with me.

Tyesha816: God please forgive me …

August 20th, 10:27 a.m.

CHAPTER 17

When I walked into the Missouri Department of Motor Vehicles, I felt the eyes of my co-workers fall on me. I'm sure they were wondering if I was coming in to work because the place was swamped. But I wasn't here to start my shift.

In order to get behind the counter, employees had to be buzzed in. I didn't want to wait so I hopped over the half door in one bound, my running shoes giving off a small squeak against the shiny tile as I landed firm on the other side.

William looked at me crazy when I took over his computer. I apologized to his customer and started typing.

"Tyesha, what are you doing?" William asked nervously.

"I'm trying to find my daughter."

William gave me more space to type. "Well hurry up," he said. "Ruth is here today but she's out on lunch. If she catches you on my computer—"

"She's gonna fire me," I finished for him, as I continued typing. "I know. And I really don't care right about now."

He whispered to me, "Yeah, she's gonna fire you. But that's not the only thing. Unauthorized access to the system is a felony and you and I both know Ruth will make sure the State presses charges against you, *after* they give you the boot. You won't be able to find your daughter while in prison."

I stopped typing, but only for a moment. I had to keep going. When I decided last night to find Ladykiller's address, I knew full well what I was doing. I knew there was a chance Ruth could catch me. Did I think about her pressing charges? No, I didn't. But as long as the police didn't catch me before I found Kylie, I didn't care. I'd do my time knowing my daughter was safe with her grandmother. And if I ended up having to kill Ladykiller, I knew

I'd be doing *a lot* of time. Those were the questions going through my head last night—*Are you willing to take his life? Will you go to prison to find your daughter? Could you live your life without her, knowing you didn't try your hardest to find her?*

Yes, yes, and NO!

"Hurry," William prompted. "She has an hour lunch and she left at eleven. If you know Ruth, you know she doesn't get back late."

I looked at the clock on the wall. It was ten till.

First, I found Gideon's address under his full name, Gideon Byers. I had called him this morning to ask for a gun. It didn't surprise me when he gave me an adamant "No." I pleaded with him, even started crying desperately, but he told me he didn't want me to go to jail in pursuit of Kylie. I understood, but I still was getting his gun. I was going to go to his house and take it. When I called him, he was at the grocery store. Hopefully I could get in and get out before he got back. And then it was on to Ladykiller's.

I clicked a pen and scribbled down the address on a sticky note. The customer sighed impatiently, and William told him it wouldn't be much longer. Then I looked up at the clock again.

I had seven minutes.

Typing in Landon Roby, Ladykiller's real name, I came up with nothing. Then I realized that he probably didn't own a car because he was only seventeen. But was he really just a teenager? I couldn't be sure. He looked like a grown man in person and even older on his profile picture.

I started over with another search, glancing at the clock. Four minutes.

My fingers moved like quick spider legs as I typed in the name the detective gave me of Ladykiller's mother. Before I could finish, though, William tapped me on the shoulder. I looked at him and then followed his eyes—which were bulging like he'd seen a ghost—toward the entrance, where I saw Ruth coming in the door sipping a soft drink through a straw.

Dammit! She's back three minutes early!

I typed faster and hit enter. Nothing came up! And then I saw that I misspelled her name. I typed it in again and then the address popped up.

"Tyesha Fenty!" Ruth called.

William buzzed her in as I finished writing down the street address. I didn't need the city, state, and zip code. But I did write down what kind of car Ladykiller's mother owned. A white BMW 325i.

As I stuffed the information in my pocket, Ruth tried to go in it when I pulled my hand out.

I slapped her hand down.

"What did you put in there?" she hissed.

"None of your fucking business," I snapped. "Don't ever put your hands on me again."

"Whatever you put in your pocket is my business. You're not even supposed to be here today. You're on leave. So anything you did on that computer is in violation of policy—and the law." She turned to William. "Did you let her on your computer?"

"No, ma'am," he said, showing his palms in his innocence.

I didn't have time for this. I tried to walk past her but she grabbed my wrist. When I tried to yank away, her frail body jumped forward but she still didn't let go.

"Bitch, I will kill you!" I shouted. "Let me go!"

"No, I'm calling the police. You're not going any-where." Then she shouted at the security guard for help. "Stuart Bradshaw, get over here and apprehend her!"

Stuart hopped the half door like I did earlier. I couldn't let him arrest me so I pulled away harder, but now Ruth had both hands locked on my wrist. I cocked back with my free hand to knock her old ass out but Stuart caught my arm by the crook of my elbow. He pulled me back away from her.

"Call the police," Ruth said to William, who imme-diately picked up his desk phone and started dialing. I wasn't mad at him for having loyalty to his job. But I was mad at Stuart for not letting me go.

"I have to get out of here!" I screamed at him, as I tried to wriggle out of his hold on my waist with no luck.

"Take her to the back, Stuart, and keep her there," Ruth commanded. "William, give me the phone and take care of this customer."

I kicked and screamed as Stuart drug me to the back of the building inside the break room. He closed the door and let me go. When I tried to go around him and back out, he pushed me back.

"Stuart, don't do this! Please! I have to find my daughter!"

Then he did the strangest thing. He extended his arm and pointed behind me.

I turned and saw the emergency exit.

"You got away from me and you escaped," he said. "I couldn't catch you."

I threw my arms around him and gave him a hug. "Thank you."

"Go find your daughter," he said.

I sprinted towards the exit and barged into the door with my shoulder, the alarm wailing as it flung open and I stumbled out into the shade of the building's rear.

CHAPTER 18

This was my first time laying eyes on Gideon's house. It was just like the rest of the houses in this neighborhood—gable to gable roof, two stories high, no garage. Modest living. It reminded me of the sort of homey house my grandmother lived in. But to my knowledge, Gideon lived alone and didn't need this much house.

Unless he was planning to start a family.

As I walked across the grass, I looked around to find the best place to break in. I couldn't do the windows because all the ones on the first level had bars on them. Gideon would be back by the time I figured out how to get those off.

I took a chance on just opening the front door. It was locked—I knew it wouldn't be that easy. Nothing in my life ever was.

I went back into the middle of the yard and stared at the house with my hands on my hips. There was a lower roof I could probably reach if I had a ladder. I didn't see one anywhere so I got in my car and parked it inches from the side of the house. I hopped back out and climbed on the trunk of my G6, then the roof, which sunk in a little under my feet. I hoisted myself up by using the gutter, and then I was on Gideon's lower roof.

I didn't look down. I stayed close to the siding until I got to the nearest window. Tugging on it, I found that it was locked too. Maybe even sealed closed from the white caulking on the window sill. It looked like it had never been opened, ever.

I'll pay you back, Gideon, I thought as I kicked the window out. I cleared the rest of the glass out with the heel of my Coach sneaker and then stepped inside.

I was in a bedroom. It was spacious, so I guessed this was the master bedroom. Right where I wanted to be. I looked under his bed for a gun but didn't find it. I checked under his pillows, in the closet, throwing off lids of shoe-boxes, checking all the places I thought thugs hid their weapons. The room was a mess when I was finished. And I was getting frustrated because I hadn't found it yet. I knew he owned a gun. And I didn't think he would take it to the grocery store with him.

Out in the hall, I put my hands on the balcony railing and looked downstairs at the living room. I didn't know if I wanted to start searching down there or try the other two rooms up here. But I was willing to tear this whole house up until I found a pistol to kill Ladykiller.

I started down the steps—and that's when I heard something.

A woman's voice coming from the basement.

"Shut up! You think you're the only one that's hungry?"

Curiously, I walked closer to the sounds.

"I said shut up!"

I accidentally stepped on something that cracked under my shoe. When I moved my foot, I squatted down to inspect it. It was a chain and locket that was terrifyingly familiar. Popping the heart-shaped locket open, I stared at a tiny picture of myself and Rodrick at prom.

My daughter was here!

In a panic, my mind tried to figure out what was going on. I reached in my pocket and looked at the addresses I had written down. I didn't put the names down with the addresses. I think I mistakenly came straight to Ladykiller's house instead of Gideon's! If I was correct, Ladykiller's mother was in the basement with my daughter!

Heart racing, I flung open the basement door.

"Deborah Roby, I know you're down there!" I shouted. "I want my daughter back and I'm not leaving until I have her!"

"Momma! Help me!"

Kylie!

Without thinking, I trotted down the steps, driven by the sweet sound of my baby girl's voice. Halfway down the steps, a hand shot out from between the steps and tripped me up. I fell to the dirty concrete of the basement. Before I could get up, I was kicked in the gut, which flipped me over onto my back. I held my stomach, cringing in pain.

"Tyesha, I don't know how you found this house," the woman taunted, "but you're gonna regret that you ever did."

I looked at the woman standing over me, not wanting to believe who I was seeing. But as hard as I squinted, the face didn't change—it was Deja Michelle.

"Momma!"

My eyes darted to Kylie and I laid eyes on her for the first time in what felt like years, but had only been a little over 24 hours. Her wrists were tied with nylon cable ties fastened to the gas pipe behind the washing machine. Strands of her brown hair were sticking up out of her little braids, her face was dingy and her fingertips were near black, but she didn't look like she'd been harmed. The whites of her eyes where still bright and innocent.

The sight of her filled me with good adrenaline. I started to push myself to my feet but Deja jabbed me in the rib with a wooden broom handle, then she yelled at my daughter to stop screaming.

"Why are you doing this?" I asked, holding my side in pain. "Why did you take my daughter?"

"You know why," she said. "This is revenge."

"What have I ever done to you, Deja? We were best friends. I loved you like a sister."

She scoffed at me. "Sister's don't steal men from each other, do they? Do you remember what you told me when I said I had a crush on Rodrick in high school? You said he wouldn't like me because he doesn't date big girls. What kind of fuckin' sister says that, huh?"

I instantly remembered the comment. It was our junior year, and we were standing by my locker when Rodrick walked past. When Deja said she liked him I had laughed and made the remark about her being too big for him. But always making references to Deja's weight was my way of helping her lose it. And looking at her now, wearing a form-fitting blue jumpsuit that she would've never been able to pull off in high school, it clearly worked.

Never had I thought I was being so harsh on her to make her want to kidnap my daughter. Looking at the pain in her eyes now, I could see she'd been holding in evil feelings about me for all these years. I felt even worse for dating Rodrick. But I hadn't believed back then that she seriously thought she had a chance of hooking up with him. And that was horrible of me.

"Deja, I'm sorry. You can have Rodrick. I didn't know—"

With both hands she jammed the broom stick in my stomach harder than before. "You think you can just *give* Rodrick to me? You can't give me shit! I *took* him, just like you took him from me. See, that's your problem. You still treat me like I'm the fat friend. Like I'm a charity case who can only be helped by you. You even take credit for how I look now. You may have exercised *with* me, but *I* put in the hard work to get my body like this."

"Deja, you're right, and I'm sorry. You look beautiful. I don't even know why you would want somebody like Rodrick. Look at you. You can do so much better than him."

She stooped down and placed the end of the broom stick on the tip of my nose. "Don't try to play mind games with me. Rodrick is a good man. *You* ruined him! He would've went to college on a football scholarship if you didn't get pregnant by him. Because of you, he had to hustle in the streets, and that's why he ended up in jail. If you hadn't stolen him from under my nose, there's no telling where me and him would be right now. But you know what, Tyesha? I'm going to make things the way they should have been. I'm going to help Rodrick be the man he was supposed to be, before you ruined his life."

"He's just gonna play you like he played me."

She smacked me across the face. "Shut up! There you go downtalking me again. He treated you like shit because you *are* shit. I am and have always been a better woman than you, even when I was at my heaviest. Rodrick respects me. Your high and mighty ass is just too stuck on yourself to see it."

"Deja, please. I just want my daughter. Let her go, please."

"She stays. You don't deserve her." She stood up, gripping the broom stick high above her head. "And people like you don't deserve to live."

Deja stabbed the broom end down at my face.

I rolled out the way and she struck the concrete. As I sprang to my feet, she lunged at me with the broom end like a javelin; I tried to duck but it caught me in the shoulder, pushing me back on my ass. Deja's momentum sent her falling on top of me.

"Kylie was supposed to be *my* daughter!" she screamed, scratching her nails into my face viciously.

Her nails burned through my skin as I tried to swat her hands away. I got ahold of one of her arms and threw her off balance, rolling her over and straddling her. I started pounding on her face with hammer fists, as I heard my daughter crying behind me—and I think her cries made me pound even harder. Deja's face grew bloody fast, almost as if the blood was seeping through her pores. I felt outside of myself; my rage had taken ahold of me again.

I grabbed two fistfuls of her hair and bashed the back of her head against the concrete over and over. She latched onto my shirt, staining it with her bloody fingers, but her grip was weak.

"Momma, he's here!"

I turned and saw my daughter looking up the stairs. Then I heard the footsteps above. *Ladykiller!*

The thought of him sent me into a panic. I hopped off of Deja and went to my daughter, trying desperately to release the ties. I bit into them but it did nothing but make my teeth ache. Still, I kept biting, and I thought I was making progress when Kylie screamed and I felt Deja's arms wrap around my neck in a suffocating hold. I fell back, fighting to get her arms off of me. Her legs wrapped around my waist and locked me against her. I was helpless.

"I've been waiting for this," Deja said through gritted teeth. She sounded like a monster. "I've had it hard my whole life. Because of you!"

Her hold tightened, crushing my wind pipe. I could hear my daughter calling to me but I couldn't see her. I was subjected to only staring at the ceiling, and it was getting very blurry.

"I wanted to be like you," she hissed. "You were always so pretty. All the boys from school still comment on your pictures; they like everything you post. But nobody notices me."

I caught a breath when I pulled on her arms but she tightened up again and I was seeing red. She squeezed harder.

"It's all gonna change when you're gone," she said in a craze. "They'll notice me. I won't be in your shadow anymore."

"Let her go, Deja. Now!"

I didn't understand it but Gideon was prying Deja's arms from around my neck. *How did he find me?*

He separated us as we got to our feet. Deja tried to attack me again but Gideon pushed her back.

"Kill her, Gideon!" Deja yelled. "What are you waiting for?"

I saw Gideon was holding a black handgun. *Kill me? Was she crazy? Gideon was my homey.*

"She's the one who kidnapped Kylie," I told him. "Her and Ladykiller did it together. And he might be on his way back." I pulled out my cell phone. "I'm calling the police."

"Give me the phone," Gideon said.

I handed it to him. When he put it on the floor and crushed it under his heel, I was speechless. Deja started laughing, her teeth bloody red, and it all became clear. I hadn't made a mistake with the addresses at all. This *was* Gideon's house. He and Deja were in cahoots.

219

"Tie her up with her daughter," Gideon said to Deja.

"No, shoot her," Deja cried. "She knows what's going on."

"Just tie her up first, Deja. Shit."

Deja pushed me toward the gas pipe and shoved me to the floor next to my daughter. She cable-tied my wrists around the pipe. Extra tight.

"We need to talk right now, Gideon," said Deja. "We can't keep both of 'em here for long."

Gideon looked at me and sighed. "It's wasn't supposed to be like this," he said to me.

Then the two of them walked up the stairs and closed the door.

CHAPTER 19

I immediately tried yanking on the ties. The pipe didn't budge one bit.

"She use *swizzers*," Kylie pronounced. "When I had to go to the *bafroom*, she cut t'em with *swizzers*."

We didn't have scissors so I started looking around me to see if I could find anything sharp within a leg's reach. I didn't see anything but lint balls and used fabric softener sheets. There were boxes on the other side of the basement but there was no way I could get over there.

"I know it's something in those boxes ..." I said to myself.

"I can get loose," Kylie said. I watched as she tried to pull her little hands out of her ties. Her thumb was bending in unnaturally and I started to tell her to stop until I saw her hand slip free. I gasped, and a second later her other hand was loose too.

"Look and see if you can find some scissors," I said.

My heart was beating fast as she scampered over and searched one of the boxes. I heard Gideon and Deja upstairs arguing and I knew it was only a matter of time before they came back down.

"We should have killed Kylie the first day we took her!" Deja yelled.

"And what would we have done with the body?" Gideon hurled back.

"Bury it!"

"Bury it where?"

"Anywhere! In the backyard."

"Are you crazy? How about we bury her in yo backyard!"

I asked Kylie did she find anything and she looked at me and shook her head no. I whispered for her to look for *anything* sharp, not just scissors. Then she ran over with a device that I was sure was going to save our lives—a cell phone.

I held the power button and said a silent prayer. It was an old cell, not a smartphone, that Gideon probably stuck in a box down here. The screen lit up and so did my eyes. Even when the display flashed "no service," I still had hope. I knew 911 could still be dialed out without minutes or a service plan. But when I pressed the "9," the screen went black. I tried to turn it back on but the battery was dead.

I told Kylie to go look for another one.

"We gotta take 'em outta state," I heard Gideon say, "like we planned to do in the first place."

"No, we have to get rid of them now!" Deja shouted.

"I told you why we can't do that. We can't kill them here. That'll be too much evidence in my basement. You're supposed to kill them where you bury them. Niggas in the joint told me this shit."

"That plan sounded good before Tyesha got here. It would've been easy to move Kylie alive because she's a little girl. Trying to take Tyesha too will get us caught. She busted my fuckin' head up. Something can go wrong on the trip there. She's a sneaky bitch, Gideon!"

"Don't call her out her name."

"Are you fucking serious?!"

In a sharp whisper, I told my daughter to hurry. She dug in a box that tipped over and spilled contents to the floor. My heart raced, waiting for one of them to come bolting down. But they kept yelling at each other. Kylie picked something up and ran over to me. It was a box cutter.

Hurriedly, I stuck the dull blade between my wrist and the zip tie. I sawed back and forth until it popped off and did the same with the other one. I went and rummaged through the boxes, looking for another phone. Instead, I found a laptop computer. It didn't look new at all—the Dell symbol was missing, and so was the "H" and the "E" on the keyboard. But it had a wireless symbol so I tried to power it on.

It worked!

Deja's voice boomed through the floor above us. "You know she has to die too now, right? Tell me you know that, Gideon!"

"So you get to be with Rodrick ... and who will I have now?"

"That's not my problem! We teamed up to get rid of their daughter. Everything was fine until your girl showed up. Now she has to die. What do you think, that she's still gonna wanna be with you?!"

This had to be the slowest computer I'd ever seen. It was still booting up. No wonder he trashed it.

"Go down there and handle your business, Gideon. Or give me the gun. I'll do it … Give me the gun, Gideon!"

There was silence upstairs, then: "Fine," Deja said. I heard her stomping across the floorboards into another part of the house. "I'll stab that bitch to death."

Then her footsteps were coming back, closer to the basement door.

I had to hurry!

"No, Deja!"

"Move, nigga!"

The home screen appeared and I clicked the internet icon. It started to buffer. I glanced up the steps, hearing them yelling at each other close to the door. When the Web finally popped up, I logged in to The Site and typed in my username and password. There was more buffering—I turned and looked up the stairs again, told Kylie to say a prayer—and then my profile page popped up. I dug the sticky note out my pocket and typed Gideon's address in without using the missing letters. Also, The Site had a navigation feature that pinpointed the exact location posts were coming from; I clicked it.

My fingers hovered over the keyboard, trying to think of a message I could post that didn't have an "H" or "E" in the spelling. I couldn't put "help me" or it would read "hlp m." I couldn't put "save me" or it would just come out as "sav m." My brain wasn't working fast enough!

Then a thought came to mind, the only thing I could think of.

Tyesha816: 349 Dnvr av CALL_ COPS!_#KIDNAP_#QUICKLY!

The basement door flung open. Me and Kylie ran back to the gas pipe and I stuffed the computer behind the washing machine. We both wrapped our arms around the pipe as if we were still tied to it. The box cutter was still in my pocket, the handle sticking out. I placed my elbow over it to conceal it.

Deja came flying down the steps. When I saw the large kitchen knife in her hand, I grabbed Kylie around the waist and was about to roll us out of the way when there was a loud blast. Deja's mouth widened in shock—and I thought she was surprised to see our arms untied, until I saw the blood pour out her mouth. She collapsed to the cracked concrete right in front of us. I quickly made Kylie hug the pipe again.

Gideon slowly trotted down the steps. When his face came into view, it was a mask of deep regret. He sat down on the last step and looked at me with sorrow in his eyes. Then he closed them, lowering his head.

I looked behind the washer and saw that I hadn't clicked "post" yet. My message was just sitting there. Secretly, I stuck my hand out and tapped enter. His head popped up and I jerked my hand back.

"I just wanted you in my life," he said to me. "That's what this was all about. She wanted Rodrick, I wanted you."

"Are you gonna kill us?" I asked him.

"I think I have to, Tyesha. It was just supposed to be your daughter. Because me and Deja knew the only thing keeping you and Rodrick together was Kylie. But then you came here and threw everything off. I knew I couldn't let Deja kill you. If anybody is gonna do it, it's gonna be me."

I glanced over at the screen. *Shit!* It was still buffering my message!

"But I don't know if I can go through with it," he continued. "I love you too much."

Confused, I said, "You don't even know me enough to love me, Gideon."

"I know *everything* about you. I know you're favorite chicken is honey barbeque. You hate horror movies. You can't sleep with the TV on at night—and me either. You love romance and watching chick flicks with a bag of caramel popcorn. On March 19th, close to midnight, you made a post that you like men with short hair better." He waved his hand over his fade. "I used to have braids, Tyesha, but I cut it for you."

I was so stunned. He lied to me about not having a Site page. Because everything he mentioned was things I posted about myself on my profile, things I didn't think people paid that much attention to. And it scared me that he knew my posts almost word for word.

The blood pooling from the hole in Deja's back streamed close to Kylie's shoe. She scooted her foot back and the path of the blood went down the drain.

"I know what you're thinking," he said. "Those are just simple things I know about you. Even though I think the simple things count, I also know about your intimate thoughts. In one of your letters you wrote to Rodrick you said all you wanted out of life was a husband, children, and a happy home. You would make your dreams whatever your husband's dreams were and support him to the fullest. You don't know how hard that hit me. I've always wanted a real woman like that."

I gasped. "He let you read my letters?"

"No. I would sneak and read them whenever he left the cell. My favorite one was the letter you sent him where you told him how you missed him being inside you, from the side with one leg in the air. I learned in that letter that you liked being touched or kissed behind the ear. I actually took that letter from him. It's in an envelope upstairs." His eyes bore into me. "I made it a point to stay in touch with Rodrick when we got out of prison. Just so I could get close to you."

"Gideon, you're crazy."

"If I'm crazy, then you're crazy if you think Rodrick will ever change. Honestly, I think we could be one big happy crazy couple. I would love you to *death*. Only if you could get over the fact that I tried to kill your daughter and realize why I did it."

Something beeped in Gideon's pocket and he started pulling out his phone. When I glanced at the computer screen I saw that my message had posted. I suddenly realized that Gideon probably had all of my status updates synced to his phone. I quickly tried to distract him.

"Gideon, I realize why you did it," I said.

He took his eyes away from his phone. "You said what?"

"I know how you feel about me. I felt it every time

you came around. But if you didn't think me and Rodrick would work, you should have waited our relationship out."

"I did wait! I waited forever! You kept going back to that fuck nigga."

"You didn't wait long enough. You kidnapped my daughter because you couldn't wait. If you knew anything about me, you'd know I like a patient man."

His eyes grew dark. He set his phone on the steps. "Don't talk to me about patience. I did seven years in prison, waiting for my turn to find a good woman. And when I found her, she was with a man that was taking advantage of her like it was a fucking sport!"

His phone beeped again and he looked down at it.

"Look at me, Gideon," I said. "I need you to look at me. Please?"

He glanced at me, then his attention went back to the phone. He picked it up and stared at the screen.

"Gideon, look at me and talk to me! I'm begging you!"

When his brow furrowed, I knew he was seeing that he had a Site notification. I looked over at the computer screen and saw that 21 people had already Liked my status update. But I didn't want them to Like it; I wanted them to call the damn police! There were five comments:

> **Rita RealSpit Gibson:** R U in trouble?
>
> **Bobby Mason:** No, her daughter is. If you see her, call the police.
>
> **Diva Lee:** Her daughter was kidnapped yesterday.
>
> **Rita RealSpit Gibson:** I know.
>
> **Shake-it Girl12:** We're praying for you, Tyesha.

I looked back at Gideon and I knew he was reading my message on his screen. His eyebrows were slanted angrily.

"What the fuck?" he uttered. Then he looked up at me and I saw hell in his eyes. "How the fuck did you just make that post?!"

He got up and stormed over to me with the pistol in his hand. He was about to shoot me until he saw the soft glow behind the washing machine. He leaned over it to see what I was hiding.

This was my only chance.

I sprang to my feet with the box cutter in hand and stabbed Gideon in the neck. He squealed, slapping his hand to his neck to stop the blood, as I grabbed my daughter's hand and tugged her up the steps. She was moving too slow so I picked her up. At the top step, Gideon pulled my foot from under me and I let go of my daughter and slammed against the dining room floor.

"Run, Kylie!" I screamed, as he yanked me back down the steps, my head bouncing against each step on the way down. Halfway, I turned over and kicked him in his chest and sent him tumbling to the concrete floor.

I scrambled back up the steps and saw Kylie struggling to turn the knob on the front door. I turned it for her, snatching it open—but it caught. The chain was on. I closed it back, fumbled with the chain and got it off, then there was a loud blast and the door's window shattered and my ears were buzzing.

Snatching Kylie off her feet, I ran into the living room as another bullet nearly took my head off. I cut around to the kitchen where Gideon, who must have took a short cut, appeared at the other end. I doubled back and ran up the stairs carrying my daughter. Needless to say, I was panting heavily at the top.

"Kylie, go in the bathroom and lock the door," I said to her. She ran inside and I heard the lock click.

Gideon was leaping up the steps. I made sure he saw me as I ran into the nearest bedroom and closed the door. I locked it and stepped back.

Gideon barged into it and the door crashed open. I screamed as he smacked me across the face with the pistol and I fell to the floor.

He stood over me and put the gun to my lips. "You stabbed me," he spit-growled in my face. "And you ran from me like you don't even know who I am. I fuckin' loved you!" He thumbed the hammer back with a *click*. I don't know if he was doing it on purpose or accidentally, but the muzzle was pressing harder and harder into my lips, making my teeth feel like they'd snap inward out of my gums. I tried to turn my face but he grabbed my chin and kept the muzzle on my mouth. "Look at me! Because this is the last face of the last man you will ever see! The face of the *only* man that loved you!"

"Wrong," said someone from behind.

Suddenly, Gideon was pulled off of me and bodyslammed against the floor. It knocked him out cold.

I should have been happy but I wasn't. I was even more terrified as I stared into the face of Ladykiller.

"I saw your message and I came to save you," he explained. "I kept driving until I saw your car on the side of the house. It's okay now." He extended his hand to help me up. "C'mon. I think I heard Kylie in the bathroom."

Hesitantly, I took his hand, and when he helped me up I kneed him square in the balls. He dropped to his knees as I raced out the room. I beat on the bathroom door.

"Kylie, open up, hurry!"

"I can't," she said from the other side, the knob rattling.

"Tyesha, I'm here to save you."

I turned. Ladykiller was walking towards me holding his crotch.

"Don't come near me!" I screamed with my back against the door. Kylie was still rattling the knob. I tried the knob myself while keeping my eyes on Ladykiller.

He got within ten feet of me when I saw Gideon appear in the doorway behind him. He shot Ladykiller in the back, twisting him around, fired again and he collapsed to the floor. Bleeding badly, Ladykiller pushed himself against the hallway wall. He stared down at the blood weeping out of his stomach, when Gideon put the gun to his head.

"So you're in love with her too, huh?" Gideon asked him.

"No," Ladykiller wheezed out.

"Why are you here then, nigga?"

"I came to save her." Ladykiller looked at me, letting out fast pants of breath. "She's my big sister."

My brow furrowed at his claim. The first thing that popped in my head was that he was lying. How could that be? Was he that delusional?

Gideon chuckled. "You hear that, Tyesha? He thinks he's your brother?"

"I am," he said. "Your father, Leeland Fenty, is my father. He got my mother pregnant, and your mother wanted nothing to do with him when she found out I was born …" He swallowed his own blood. "I just wanted to meet you,

Tyesha … to be your friend. I wanted to meet my niece. But your mother wanted me to stay away from you."

My mouth dropped in shock. I could see the striking resemblance now between Ladykiller and my father. Their dark brown eyes were unmistakably the same. No wonder I had an uneasy feeling the first time I saw him. All my life my mother had kept to herself about the true reason surrounding why she left my father. All I knew was that he was a cheater, but I knew deep down there was something more she was hiding from me.

"Well I'll be damned," Gideon said. "I guess I wasn't the only man that loved you, Tyesha." He stepped back and aimed down at Ladykiller with precision. "But I am now."

"No!" I screamed. Without thinking, I charged toward Gideon. He swung the gun at me as I plunged into him.

We broke the wood railing and fell together, smacking the hardwood below. The fall banged us both up—me a lot more. I could barely move and my vision was blurry but I saw Gideon already crawling over the broken pieces of the railing toward the gun.

Then the front door opened and let in blinding light.

"Hello?" the woman who stuck her head in asked. "Tyesha?"

Gideon paused, but only for a moment. He crawled faster toward the weapon but the woman at the door quickly picked it up and pointed it at him.

"Don't move, motherfucker," she said to him. "Tyesha, I'm Rita Gibson. Are you okay?"

Tyesha816: Thank you to everybody who showed me support in finding my daughter! She's HOME!—*with* **Rita RealSpit Gibson, Ladykiller,** *and* **4 others**.

September 1st, 8:00 a.m.

CHAPTER 20

Momma bounced back and forth from the stove to the sink, preparing another one of her famous meals. I was leaning against the doorway of the kitchen, occasionally glancing up at her between reading the comments on my phone from the status update I made this morning. It took me over a week to make another post. I didn't want anything to do with The Site. I was too busy spending time with my daughter. But I had missed the interaction with my internet family—the ones that supported me, anyway—and I knew I wouldn't be able to hold out for long.

Quita Wheeler: I had faith that you would find her!

Diedra Murberry: I'm glad she's home. I hurt every day she was gone.

Atlanta Baby: Give that pretty girl a hug for me!

Project Life (Patrick Henson): Now I know why white people keep they kids on leashes. I just bought one for my son.

Tyesha816: @Project Life. I think I might head to Target tonight! Lol!

Lataya GrindGirl: God is good all the time!

Renae MyPerogative Watson: The whole time she was gone I couldn't sleep. I couldn't imagine how you felt. Thank you for posting that she's home. Now I might be able to get some rest.

God's Angel: ^^same here.

Rita RealSpit Gibson: We all have trials and tribulations in our life that are hard to face alone. We all need support, even if it's from people we barely know or don't know at all.

Tyesha816: @Rita RealSpit Gibson. Me and my daughter wouldn't be here today if it wasn't for your concern and courage. I can't thank you and @Ladykiller enough.

Rita RealSpit Gibson: I don't know if it was so much as courage or instincts. Would I have pulled the trigger if he made a move? I'm glad we didn't have to find out.

It wasn't just Ladykiller and Rita RealSpit Gibson that showed up at Gideon's house to help me. There were four others that found the house right before the police showed up—Christina "MsFineGirl" Irving, Joanne Dunley and Stuart Bradshaw, and Marley "Fedbound" Dubois. I personally thanked them all on their profile pages.

"So who's the special guest?" my mother asked me, as I took my eyes away from my phone.

"You'll see. He's in the dining room at the table, ready to eat."

"He?" Momma's lips formed an "O," and her eyebrows lifted in excitement. She whispered, "You brought over a new man?"

"Yes, I did."

"Any man has to be better than that Rodrick. I'm glad you finally saw the light."

"Momma, who I brought over isn't somebody I'm dating."

"No need to explain," she said, cutting me off. She shoved the bowl of salad into my hands. "You're friends, I get it. He's probably hungry. Let him get started on that while I finish up the beef. He does eat beef, right?"

"Yes, ma'am."

We waited in the dining room with eager smiles on our faces—me, Kylie, and Landon Roby, aka Ladykiller. Well, Ladykiller's smile seemed a bit more nervous than eager. He was at the head of the table in a wheelchair.

He whispered to me, "I don't know if this is a good idea?"

"Why?"

"Last time I was here, she kicked me off of her property."

"That was then. This is now. I think she was just trying to protect me from knowing—"

Glass shattering startled us. Momma had dropped the plate of croissants right when she entered the dining room. Her face was full of shock and disbelief.

"What's going on?" she asked.

"Uncle *La'killer* is here," Kylie chirped.

It looked like Momma was angry. I swallowed and said, "I invited Landon over for dinner."

"Only family eats at my house on Sundays," she said in a dark tone. "You know that, Tyesha. I didn't let Rodrick eat here and I'm not letting *him* eat here either. Show him to the door."

"Momma, he is fam—"

"No, he's not!" she yelled. "He's not a part of this family. He's a mistake."

"How could you say that? He's my brother."

She shook her head violently. "No! If he didn't come out of me, he's NOT your brother!"

"Really?" I raised my voice. "I had gotten over the fact that you didn't accept Rodrick. But I'm seeing now that you won't accept anybody, if it's not within your perfect little lie you choose to live in. Momma, I'm not perfect, daddy wasn't perfect, and neither are you."

"Don't talk to me like that!"

"I remember when Kylie was born. You refused to come to the hospital to see her just because I had her out of wedlock."

"Stop it," she seethed.

"But over time you learned to love her," I went on. "Please don't push Landon away. We have the same flesh and blood. He *is* my brother. And he saved my life."

"Get him out of my house right now!"

I let out a mean breath like a bull, then grabbed the back of Landon's wheelchair. "Come on, Kylie." I wheeled him outside, bumping down the concrete steps.

He hit the hand brake.

"I'm sorry," he said. He blinked, and two tears trickled down his cheeks. "My mother is the same way. She didn't want me trying to get in touch with you. But I always wanted to meet you and get to know my other family. I'm sorry for not going about it a different way."

He lowered his head and started crying. I kissed him on the cheek and put my arms around him.

"I don't care how you got in touch with me. I'm just glad you did. We can start our own tradition. Waffle House, every Sunday. How you like that?"

He smiled wistfully. "That sounds good."

Kylie's little arms wrapped around us, too.

"Oh," he said suddenly. "Since we're going somewhere else to eat, I have a question?"

"What is it?"

"Can I bring my daughters?"

I gasped. "You have children?"

"Yep. My oldest daughter is two, and her birthday is a day after Kylie's. My youngest is nine months. Two different baby mommas. Yo little brother has a way with the ladies. That's why they call me Ladykiller."

I cracked up laughing. "Oh my God! I can't wait to meet them."

"Me too," Kylie said.

251

Tyesha816 listed **Ladykiller** as her brother.

CHAPTER 21

The guards wouldn't let inmates touch the money, so I had to place nine quarters into the vending machine myself. When the turtle cake fell, Rodrick hunkered down and grabbed it out of the slot.

"Do you want a drink?" he asked me nicely, as if he were paying.

"No. Do you want one?"

"Yeah. Get me a Pepsi."

Thankfully, the State never brought back up the murder case against Rodrick. But he still had to do time for his parole violation for coming in contact with the police without notifying his parole officer. I couldn't believe that was actually a parole rule, but it was. Rodrick said there were endless rules to keep felons in a "closed circuit of perpetual marginality"—whatever that meant. At the most, he'd have to do six more months. But for Kylie's sake, hopefully the board would give him an early review.

We sat down in plastic chairs at our table. Kylie was behind us in the visiting room's play area, building a Lego house with a girl close to her age. I unwrapped my burrito and took a bite.

"I have to ask you something, Rodrick."

"Wussup?"

"Did I mess up your life?"

He looked confused. "How could you do that?"

"By getting pregnant. You had a good future ahead of you with the basketball scholarship and everything. I remember you started hustling after that to take care of Kylie. I know if I would have never gotten pregnant, you would probably be playing pro. I always wondered if that's why you cheated on me so much ... because you resented me."

"You got it all wrong. I started hustling before I found out you was pregnant. And when I did find out, that just made me hustle that much harder. Then I got busted and they took the scholarship away when I got convicted. But that's my fault. And you had a scholarship to Clark Atlanta. You turned that down to raise Kylie in Kansas City. I could be to blame for you only being able to get your associate's from that online course. Who knows how far you would've went if you had gone to Atlanta. To be honest, I started trying to get you pregnant when I found out you got yo scholarship. I figured you was about to do big things and I wanted to keep you, get you pregnant before one of them niggas down there did. So I'm sorry for doing *you* wrong."

"Thank you for saying that."

"I didn't cheat because I resented you. I cheated because I was stupid. When I got out of prison the first time, I felt like I owed every female that sent me a letter. Fuckin' all of 'em was my way of saying thank you. You know how appreciative I am, Tyesha. But that was a twisted, selfish way of thinking. I've since learned from my mistakes. That's why I stopped that cheating shit."

"You stopped? When?"

One of the guards walked up and told me to keep my hands visible on the table. He also made Rodrick tuck in his prison red shirt and hand over the rubberband holding up his dreads. Rubberbands weren't allowed.

"I been done stopped," Rodrick told me when the guard walked off. "And not just since I got locked up again."

"You'll never change, Rodrick. I've learned that some people never will. You can't force people to change; the only person you can change is yourself. The only reason I came up here was so you could see your daughter. And to tell you that I'm moving on."

"Hold up, Tyesha. I just told you that I stopped cheating."

"That's funny. Because the one bitch I just knew you would never talk to again, Dava Babcock, just posted a picture of a letter you sent her two days ago. And before you fix your face to tell a lie, let me ad lib what the letter said. '*Dear Dava, I can't wait till I get out so I can suck on that juice box again. I promise you I'll put it on you harder than before. No, you don't have to worry about me getting out and getting with my baby momma. Me and her are just friends. She's coming to see me Saturday just so I can see my daughter, but I got you on the list for Sunday.*

Thanks for the bread. A nigga been eatin' good in here. If the board calls me for that review, I'll be home before our baby is born. You just make sure you eat right and keep your Temple healthy and nutritious." Clearing my throat to stop myself from crying, I said, "I would be able to tell you what the rest of the letter said but the guards wouldn't let me bring in my phone. But it sure did look like your handwriting and your scribbly-ass signature."

He leaned back in his seat and sighed.

We really didn't have much to talk about for the rest of the visit. He asked to take a picture with Kylie and I didn't mind. I paid for three images and stood behind the photographer as they posed together.

"When's the next time you coming up?" he asked me.

"I don't know," I said. "But I'll try to bring Kylie at least once a month."

When I got back to my car, I buckled Kylie in her booster seat. I got in behind the wheel and checked the comments from The Site on my phone. Earlier I had up-loaded pictures of me and Kylie and Landon—and his two little girls, Kendal and Kayla—posing in front of Kaleidoscope's glass doors at Crown Center. Landon made a comment that he was glad he didn't get arrested this time. I laughed and clicked Like.

The private message box in the corner of my display screen was lit.

I tapped it with my thumb and read the message that appeared.

Rick Myers: I'll be waiting patiently until the next time I can see you again.

The message was sent to me thirty minutes ago from Cameron, Missouri. I knew Gideon Byers was locked up for 25 years in a maximum security prison in that town. "Rick Myers" was his fake Site name, which he'd been using all this time to stalk and spy on me. If he sent this message, it meant that he'd smuggled a cell phone into the institution somehow.

My first thought was to go to my settings and block him from viewing my page. But then I decided to let him keep watching. I knew one day I'd find a good man and start a family, and I wanted Gideon to see every step, to suffer every time I posted how happy I was, to get angry when I uploaded my wedding photos, to cry when he saw our child's beautiful face.

For him—but more importantly for myself—I was determined to live a blessed life. And to move forward, first I had to swallow my pride and take a step back.

Tyesha816 went from **in a relationship** to **single**.

The following is an excerpt from:

STATUS 2

CHAPTER 1

It took two hours for me and my daughter to get here. Normally, she wouldn't even be able to sit still for twenty minutes, but I kept her occupied with a new Disney movie on my smartphone.

We pulled into the prison parking lot, tires crunching over patches of snow. Rodrick told me ahead of time not to park in the same spot as usual, and I didn't. I drove straight to the end of the lot where the big gate was. There were other people standing outside their cars in big coats and skull caps, waiting on their loved ones to be released. Me and Kylie parked and joined them.

"If you get cold," I said to her, "you can get back in the car."

"I'm fine," Kylie said happily.

I smiled. She couldn't wait to hug her daddy outside of prison walls. The whole time he'd been down she would ask when he was coming home. She had the countdown on her calendar.

A guard stepped outside of one of the side buildings. "They'll be out in just a moment, people," he said. "When you see them come out, do not run up to the gate. I repeat, DO NOT run up to the gate. If you do, you just might be shot down. They'll cross the parking lot and come to you. Thank you for your cooperation." He stepped back inside.

"Asshole," said a young white woman on the side of me.

"Amen," I agreed.

"Are you here to pick up your husband?" she asked me.

"Oh no. I'm not married."

"I've been married to this man about to walk out for six years. I met him and married him while he's been locked up. We've only known each other through visits and letters, and today will mark the day we get to spend the rest of our lives together. I have butterflies. I can't keep still."

"I know how you feel. Congratulations."

It reminded me of the first time Rodrick walked out of MCC in Moberly, Missouri. It was his first time down, and he'd promised me he was going to get out and get on his feet and marry me as soon as he was financially able to. I was just as giddy and excited as the woman next to me.

But the marriage proposal never came. Only lies and betrayal.

I wasn't looking for anything from Rodrick Brown this time. All I wanted for him to do was take care of his daughter.

My phone beeped in my pocket. I had to take one of my mittens off to tap the touchscreen. I had a text message from my unofficial boyfriend. I liked to call him my "man friend."

Fedbound Marley: Where you at?

Tyesha816: I just got to Moberly.

Fedbound Marley: Oh

Tyesha816: What did you want?

Then my phone started ringing. I picked it up.

"Hey, honey," I said.

"Wussup, cute buns. I just wanted to know if you wanted to go out to see a movie tonight. Me, you, and Kylie. I
didn't know you were going to see him today. You'll probably be too tired when you get back to Kansas City, huh?"

"Yeah, not tonight. Maybe tomorrow."

He paused. "You okay? You don't sound good."

I couldn't tell him the truth. I couldn't tell him that Rodrick was being released today and I was here to pick him
up. Actually, that information probably wouldn't even get
him that upset, but when he found out that Rodrick would
be living with me because he had nowhere else to home-
plan to, I know that would get under Marley's skin. And
Marley wasn't even the type of person to get outrageously
mad, but I know I would see it in his actions—he'd probably stop calling me as much, he might not come over
again, I'd have to go over to his place. Rodrick living with
me was only going to be temporary, though. Hopefully me
and Marley's unofficial relationship—we both agreed to

keep our Site status on "single"—could hold strong long enough.

"I'm fine," I said. "It's just cold out here."

"Well, don't let me hold you up. Tell him I said wussup."

"Yeah right."

He laughed and then we hung up.

The white woman started clapping loudly. "They're opening the gate!"

I watched as a line of inmates dressed in street clothes filed out of the building on the other side of the fence. The white lady waved at a Black man with dreads in his hair, and I turned to her with a look of horror, until she said his name.

"Hi, Howard! I love you!"

I shook my head and let out a sigh of relief. It wasn't Rodrick.

He was the last one to come out of the building. His dreads were a lot longer than the other guy's. He had on the clothes that he told me to send him for his coming home dress-outs—a black pea coat, some kind of Vintage for the Vain tee that he must have seen in a magazine, black slacks and matching Louis Vuitton loafers. He looked like he owned the prison, and I'm sure that was the look he was going for.

"Daddy!" beamed Kylie.

I had to hold on to her to keep her from running across the parking lot. When he got near, I let her go and he swooped her up in his arms.

"Oh, I missed you so much, baby girl," he said to her with tears in his eyes.

I felt tears coming to my own eyes. I batted them back.

He walked over to me with our daughter on his hip. "Hey, Momma," he said.

"I parked right down there," I replied without emotion.

"Okay. We'll leave in just a moment."

When he set Kylie down, I thought he was about to ask me for a hug. But he didn't. His Black butt got down on one knee.

Oh my God!

He reached in his coat pocket and pulled out a white ring. It looked like he made it out of toilet paper, soaked in water and hardened into a tiny circle. The tears started coming down my cheeks. This couldn't be happening!

"Will you marry me?" Rodrick asked.

The other families standing around us began to gasp and clap in celebration.

"Yes!" Kylie exclaimed.

Everybody laughed, including me.

www.felonybooks.com

54233138R00171

Made in the USA
San Bernardino, CA
11 October 2017